Caribbean Stories

Longman Imprint Books
General Editor: Michael Marland

Titles in the series
There is a Happy Land Keith Waterhouse
Nine African Stories Doris Lessing
The Experience of Colour *edited by* Michael Marland
Flesh Wounds David Holbrook
The Human Element and other stories Stan Barstow
The Leaping Lad and other stories Sid Chaplin
Z Cars Four television scripts
Steptoe and Son Four television scripts
Conflicting Generations Five television scripts
A Sillitoe Selection Alan Sillitoe
Late Night on Watling Street and other stories Bill Naughton
Black Boy Richard Wright
One Small Boy Bill Naughton
The Millstone Margaret Drabble
Fair Stood the Wind for France H.E. Bates
A Way of Life and other stories Dan Jacobson
Scene Scripts Seven television plays
The Experience of Work *edited by* Michael Marland
Breaking Away *edited by* Marilyn Davies *and* Michael Marland
The Kraken Wakes John Wyndham
A Hemingway Selection Ernest Hemingway
Friends and Families *edited by* Eileen *and* Michael Marland
Ten Western Stories *edited by* C.E.J. Smith
The Good Corn and other stories H.E. Bates
The Experience of Sport *edited by* John L. Foster
Loves, Hopes, and Fears *edited by* Michael Marland
The African Queen C.S. Forester
A Casual Acquaintance and other stories Stan Barstow
Eight American Stories *edited by* D.L. James
Cider with Rosie Laurie Lee
The L-Shaped Room Lynne Reid Banks
Softly, Softly Five television scripts by Elwyn Jones
The Pressures of Life Four television plays
The Experience of Prison *edited by* David Ball
Saturday Night and Sunday Morning Alan Sillitoe
A John Wain Selection John Wain
Jack Schaefer and the American West Jack Schaefer
Goalkeepers are Crazy Brian Glanville
A James Joyce Selection James Joyce
Out of the Air Five radio plays, *edited by* Alfred Bradley
Could it be? *edited by* Michael Marland
The Minority Experience *edited by* Michael Marland and Sarah Ray
Scene Scripts Two Five television plays
Caribbean Stories *edited by* Michael Marland

Companion cassettes, with readings of some of the key stories are available for the following:
The Leaping Lad and other stories
The Human Element
A Sillitoe Selection
Late Night on Watling Street
A Casual Acquaintance
Loves, Hopes, and Fears
A John Wain Selection

LONGMAN IMPRINT BOOKS

Caribbean Stories

fifteen short stories by writers from the Caribbean

edited by
Michael Marland C.B.E., B.A. *Headmaster,*
Woodberry Down School, London

with a sequence of photographs

Longman

LONGMAN GROUP LIMITED
London

Associated companies, branches and representatives
throughout the world.

This edition © Longman Group Ltd 1978

This edition first published 1978

ISBN 0 582 23351 8

Printed in Hong Kong by
Bright Sun Printing Press Co Ltd

Contents

A Note to the Reader   page vi

Michael Anthony   **Drunkard of the River**   1
Jan Carew   **Hunters and Hunted**   6
Barnabas J. Ramon-Fortune   **The Tallow Pole**   17
John Hearne   **A Village Tragedy**   22
Ismith Khan   **The Red Ball**   34
Roger Mais   **Blackout**   42
V.S. Naipaul   **The Enemy**   46
V.S. Naipaul   **The Baker's Story**   55
V.S. Naipaul   **The Raffle**   65
H. Orlando Patterson   **The Visitor**   69
Clifford Sealy   **The Bitter Choice**   73
Karl Sealy   **My Fathers Before Me**   80
Samuel Selvon   **Cane is Bitter**   86
Samuel Selvon   **A Drink of Water**   98
Enrique Serpa   **Shark Fins**   106

Maps of the Caribbean   113
The Caribbean: a sequence of photographs   115
Points for Discussion and Suggestions for Writing   138
The Authors   144
The West Indies: a brief historical note   147
Further Reading   150
Acknowledgements   152

A Note to the Reader

These fifteen stories show people making their lives, facing difficulties, — sometimes disappointed, sometimes successful, often disagreeing, sometimes doing funny things. We read of families, and the difficulties and pleasures of parents and children; we read of the struggle to keep alive against the harshness of nature; of the problems of earning a living; of the tensions of living together with different kinds of people. In fact, these are fifteen vivid snapshots of what it is like to be human.

All the authors of the stories in this collection are from the West Indian islands of the Caribbean sea – the places shown on the map on page 114 – and the events of the stories take place in the authors' home countries.

The stories, however, have been chosen simply as fifteen stories likely to interest the student reader and to be worth close reading and attention. There is no attempt either to picture the full range of life in the Caribbean, or to represent the full range of authors of merit. In fact, the selection of authors does give a reasonable cross-section of modern Caribbean writing, but leaves out some important authors (such as Edgar Mittelholzer and V.S. Reid) because they did not happen to write short stories or because their stories did not appear to be among the most suitable for readers of this volume.

There are times in the literary life of a country when there is a powerful surge of creativity. After the Second World War such a movement swept across the West Indies, and there was a huge outpouring of new writing. It was as if the social and political changes were partly prompted by and partly led to this outburst of writing, most of which explores the life the authors knew in their various countries. Many of these writers studied abroad, and some even stayed to work abroad. But they wrote out of their experiences, and they portrayed Caribbean life. Many returned to teach or to work (often as teachers in the University of the West Indies) and to contribute to the new independent life of those countries.

There are certain major themes in the collection, especially three: the family, the struggle against nature, and the social tensions of different racial groups. However, I have arranged the stories simply in alphabetical order of authors so that readers can choose their own sequence. I hope that many readers will go on to explore the other writings of these authors, and, indeed, other Caribbean writers. I have therefore included a selected list of Further Reading on page 150.

M.M.

Drunkard of the River

Michael Anthony *(Trinidad)*

"Where you' father?"

The boy did not answer. He paddled his boat carefully between the shallows, and then he ran the boat alongside the bank, putting his paddle in front to stop it. Then he threw the rope round the picket and helped himself on to the bank. His mother stood in front the door still staring at him.

"Where you' father?"

The boy disguised his irritation. He looked at his mother and said calmly, "You know Pa. You know where he is."

"And ah did tell you not to come back without 'im?"

"I could bring Pa back?" The boy cried. His bitterness was getting the better of him. "When Pa want to drink I could bring him back?"

It was always the same. The boy's mother stood in front of the door staring up the river. Every Saturday night it was like this. Every Saturday night Mano went out to the village and drank himself helpless and lay on the floor of the shop, cursing and vomiting until the Chinaman was ready to close up. Then they rolled him outside and heaven knows, maybe they even spat on him.

The boy's mother stared up the river, her face twisted with anger and distress. She couldn't go up the river now. It would be hell and fire if she went. But Mano had to be brought home. She turned to see what the boy was doing. He had packed away the things from the shopping bag and he was now reclining on the settee.

"You have to go for you' father, you know," she said.

"Who?"

"You!"

"Not me!"

"Who de hell you tellin' not me," she shouted. She was furious now. "Dammit, you have to go for you' father!"

Sona had risen from the settee on the alert. His mother hardly ever hit him now but he could never tell. It had been a long time since she had looked so angry and had stamped her feet.

He rose slowly and reluctantly and as he glanced at her he couldn't understand what was wrong with her. He couldn't see why she bothered about his father at all. For his father was stupid and worthless and made their life miserable. If he could have had his way Mano would have been out of the house a long time now. His bed would have been the dirty meat-table in front of Assing's shop. That was what he deserved. The rascal! The boy spat through the window. The very thought of his father sickened him.

Yet with Sona's mother it was different. The man she had married and who had turned out badly was still the pillar of her life. Although he had piled up grief after grief, tear after tear, she felt lost and drifting without him. To her he was as mighty as the very Ortoire that flowed outside. She remembered that in his young days there was nothing any living man could do that he could not.

In her eyes he was still young. He did not grow old. It was she who had aged. He had only turned out badly. She hated him for the way he drank rum and squandered the little money he worked for. But she did not mind the money so much. It was seeing him drunk. She knew when he arrived back staggering how she would shake with rage and curse him, but even so, how inside she would shake with the joy of having him safe and home.

She wondered what was going on at the shop now. She wondered if he was already drunk and helpless and making a fool of himself.

With Sona, the drunkard's son, this was what stung more than ever. The way Mano, his father, cursed everybody and made a fool of himself. Sometimes he had listened to his father and he had felt to kick him, so ashamed he was. Often in silence he had shaken his fist and said, "One day, ah'll – ah'll ... "

He had watched his mother put up with hell and sweat and starvation. She was getting skinnier every day, and she looked more like fifty-six than the thirty-six she was. Already her hair was greying. Sometimes he had looked at her and, thinking of his father, he had ground his teeth and had said, "Beast!" several times to himself. He was in that frame of mind now. Bitter and reluctant, he went to untie the boat.

"If I can't bring 'im, I'll leave 'im," he said angrily.

"Get somebody to help you!"

He turned to her. "Nobody wouldn't help me. He does insult everybody. Last week Bolai kick him."

"Bolai kick 'im? An' what you do?"

His mother was stung with rage and shock. Her eyes were large and red and watery.

The boy casually unwound the rope from the picket. "What I do?" he said. "That is he and Bolai business."

His mother burst out crying.

"What ah must do?" the boy said. "All the time ah say, 'Pa, come home, come home, Pa!' You know what he tell me? He say, 'Go to hell, yuh little bitch!'"

His mother turned to him. Beads of tears were still streaming down the sides of her face.

"Sona, go for you' father. Go now. You stand up dey and watch Bolai kick you' father and you ent do nothing? He mind you, you know," she sobbed. "He is you' father, you ungrateful – – –" And choking with anger and grief she burst out crying again.

When she raised her head, Sona was paddling towards midstream, scowling, avoiding the shallows of the river.

True enough there was havoc in Assing's shop. Mano's routine was well under way. He staggered about the bar dribbling and cursing and yet again the Chinaman spoke to him about his words, not that he cared about Mano's behaviour. The rum Mano consumed made quite a difference to Assing's account. It safe-guarded Mano's free speech in the shop.

But the customers were disgusted. All sorts of things had happened on Saturday nights through Mano's drunkenness. There was no such thing as buying in peace once Mano was there.

So now with trouble looming, the coming of Sona was sweet relief. As Sona walked in, someone pointed out his father between the sugar bags.

"Pa!"

Mano looked up. "What you come for?" he drawled. "Who send you?"

"Ma say to come home," Sona said. He told himself that he mustn't lose control in front of strangers.

"Well!"

"Ma send me for you."

"You! You' mother send you for me! So you is me father now, eh – eh?" In his drunken rage the old man staggered towards his son.

Sona didn't walk back. He never did anything that would make him feel stupid in front of a crowd. But before he realised what was

3

happening his father lunged forward and struck him on his left temple.

"So you is me father, eh? You is me father, now!" He kicked the boy.

Two or three people bore down on Mano and held him off the boy. Sona put his hands to his belly where his father had just kicked him. Tears came to his eyes. The drunkenness was gripping Mano more and more. He could hardly stand on his own now. He was struggling to set himself free. The men held on to him. Sona kept out of the way.

"It's a damn' shame!" somebody said.

"Shame?" Mano drawled. "An' he is me father now, 'e modder send him for me. Let me go," he cried, struggling more than ever, "I'll kill 'im. So help me God, I'll kill 'im!"

They hadn't much to do to control Mano at this stage. His body was supple and weak now, as if his bones were turning to water. The person who had cried, "It's a damn' shame!" spoke again.

"Why you don't carry 'im home, boy? You can't see 'e only making botheration?"

"You'll help me put 'im in the boat?" Sona asked. He looked unruffled now. He seemed only concerned with getting his father out of the shop, and out of all this confusion. Nobody could tell what went on below the calmness of his face. Nobody could guess that hate was blazing in his mind.

Four men and Sona lifted Mano and carted him into the boat. The old man was snoring, in a state of drunkenness. It was the state of drunkenness when things were at rest.

The four men pushed the boat off. Sona looked at his father. After a while he looked back at the bridge. Everything behind was swallowed by the darkness. "Pa," the boy said. His father groaned. "Pa, yuh going home," Sona said.

The wilderness of mangroves and river spread out before the boat. They were alone. Sona was alone with Mano, and the river and the mangroves and the night, and the swarms of alligators below. He looked at his father again. "Pa, so you kick me up then, eh?" he said.

Far into the night Sona's mother waited. She slept a little on one side, then she turned on the other side, and at every sound she woke up, straining her ears. There was no sound of the paddle on water. Surely the shops must have closed by now, she thought.

Everything must have closed by this time. She lay there anxious and listened until her eyes shut again in an uneasy sleep.

She was awakened by the creaking of the bedroom floor. Sona jumped back when she spoke.

"Who that – Mano?"

"Is me, Ma," Sona said.

His bones, too, seemed to be turning liquid. Not from drunkenness, but from fear. The lion in him had changed into a lamb. As he spoke his voice trembled.

His mother didn't notice. "All you now, come?" she said. "Where Mano?"

The boy didn't answer. In the darkness he took down his things from the nails.

"Where Mano?" his mother cried out.

"He out there sleeping. He drunk."

"The bitch!" his mother said, getting up and feeling for the matches.

Sona quickly slipped outside. Fear dazed him now and he felt dizzy. He looked at the river and he looked back at the house and there was only one word that kept hitting against his mind: Police!

"Mano!" he heard his mother call to the emptiness of the house. "Mano!"

Panic-stricken, Sona fled into the mangroves and into the night.

Hunters and Hunted

Jan Carew *(Guyana)*

Old man Doorne and his two elder sons walked through the swamp with the ease of men who had known the feel of mud and water all their lives. But Tonic, the youngest, splashed and stumbled every now and then. The afternoon sun, fierce and yellowing, flung shadows behind them long as fallen coconut palms. The old man was carrying his *wareshi*, an Amerindian[1] haversack. His back was arched and the harness bit into his forehead and shoulders.

Ahead of them was Black Bush, a belt of dense forest which rolled inland like a green ocean. Leading into Black Bush was a sandy plain where the sun had consumed and the wind swept away all but a few clumps of grass and black sage.

They approached a reed bed where bisi-bisi and wild cane had jostled the lotus lilies out of the way.

"Is how much farther we got to go?" Tonic asked plaintively.

"Don't ask stupid question, Boy, save you breath for the walk," Doorne said.

"Nobody didn't beg you to come, so why you crying out with strain now? You, self, say you want to hunt. If you want to play man-game, then you got to take man-punishment," Caya, the eldest, said. His brother's whining angered him. It reminded him of his own tiredness.

"Ah! Lef him alone! The boy young and this swamp got teeth enough to bite the marrow of you bone out of you," Tengar growled from deep inside his belly and he added gently, "If you get too fatigue, boy, I will carry you over the last stretch."

"No!" Old man Doorne shouted. "Let the boy walk it on he own. I don't want no rice-pap mother's boy growing up under me roof." And he turned round and glared up at his second son who towered over him like a giant mora tree over a gnarled lignum vitae.

The rise and fall of their voices and the plop-plop of their feet sounded unreal in the silence. Far to their right negrocups, swamp

[1] *Amerindian*: similar to those used by the original inhabitants of the islands.

6

birds of the heron family, were grazing near a cluster of lilies. The birds stretched long necks to gaze at the intruders. A flock of ducks and curry-curries rose noisily from the bisi-bisi reeds ahead of them. But the negrocups stood moving their heads from side to side nervously and preening their wings for flight. The horizon behind those ostrich-like birds was a circle of mirages where the hazy green swamps melted away, calcinated by the sun before they merged with the sky.

As the old man and his sons drew nearer Black Bush they saw the jungle where tall trees, massed growths of bamboo and closely woven tapestries of vines and creepers had erupted out of the earth. The sight put Doorne in a good mood. In the middle of the bamboo grove was a dark hole: it was almost blocked up by new shoots but the old man recognised it. He had cut it out himself on his last trip. Huge yellow and blue butterflies danced before it. Against the dark background their wings were incandescent.

"Come on, Tonic, only lil' way to go now, boy. Brace yourself against the mud, keep you foot wide apart to fight it," Doorne said.

"Is how much farther we got to go?" Tonic asked again and his voice was listless like a man with fever.

"Don't worry, Small-boy, I will carry you over the las' stretch," Tengar said, stopping to hoist his brother on his broad back.

"Lef the boy alone, Tengar!" the old man said fiercely. "He got to learn to be a hunter. Even if he bright like moonlight on still water, is time he understand he can't live by book alone. He too black and ugly to be a book man."

"The boy is you son, old man, but he is me brother," Tengar said.

Tonic, his legs round Tengar's waist and his hands locked around his neck, looked like a black spider clinging to a tree trunk.

"Put the boy down!" Doorne insisted, blocking Tengar's path.

"Move out the way, old man, and stop making gar-bar,"[2] Tengar said, still good-natured.

"Put the boy down!" Doorne shouted, whipping out his prospecting knife.

"Old man, don't look for trouble, because when you searching for it that is the time it does ambush you. Don't bank on me vexation jus' staying in me belly and rupturing me, jus' because

[2]*gar-bar*: trouble.

7

we is the same flesh and blood."

Caya stepped between them and said, "All you two making mirth or what? Look, stop this fool-acting. Old man, you better put you knife away. If the small boy too weak to bear the strain is you fault. You encourage he to full-up he head with white man book and all of we does boast how he going to turn doctor or lawyer. When turtle papa give he shell, nobody can change it.'

Growling and muttering, Doorne sheathed his knife and Tengar moved on.

"Thank you, brother Tengar," Tonic whispered and the black giant grinned showing white teeth between well-fleshed lips.

Doorne's face looked like a sky threatening rain. He thrust his head forward and strode on.

A hundred yards from dry land, Caya burst out singing:

> "Kaloo, kaloo,
> Lef' me echo in the bush las' time.
> Was sundown when wind steal that echo of mine.
> Kaloo, kaloo,
> Sundown wind steal me echo
> And I tell Wind leggo me echo! Leggo!
> But wind wouldn't set me echo free.
> Wind hide me echo in the bowel of a tree.
> Wind wouldn't set me echo free.
> Kaloo, kaloo.
> A who-you bird set me echo free
> A who-you bird steal it from the tree.
> Kaloo, kaloo."

Caya sang with a deep bass voice and because this was their way of celebrating another victory over the swamps, the others joined in the chorus:

> "A who-you bird set me echo free
> A who-you bird steal it from the tree.
> Kaloo, kaloo."

Tengar made Tonic walk the last fifty yards and Doorne, although he pretended not to notice, understood that this was done to placate him. The gesture, however, irritated the old man.

"Eh, eh, you get so weak you can't carry you fly-weight brother couple yards," he jeered.

Tengar did not answer his father. Other people's malice was something he could never understand; that it should linger and rankle always baffled him. Perhaps it was his father's vindictive Amerindian blood, he thought.

Tonic staggered across the last stretch of water and as he forced his way through bisi-bisi and wild cane reeds, they tossed as if a storm had hit them. Looking at his brother, Caya burst out laughing.

"Go on, Tonic, go on. Go on, mother's boy," he said.

"Ah, leave the small boy alone," Tengar said.

"Papa Tengar and he boy-child," Doorne taunted.

Tonic crawled up on dry land and lay down, his feet still trailing in the swamp.

"But is why I come on this brute-walk?" he sobbed.

"We tell you wasn't fun; this swamp got teeth boy," Caya said.

"You only full of 'I tell you this' and 'I tell you the other,' but how was I to know that this sun was so hot, that this swamp would be me kinnah?" [3]

"All right, Boy, all right. You hold out well enough," Doorne said, lifting him up and putting him on higher ground.

Against the whiteness of Tonic's eyeballs the brown irises were luminous. His face had the dark sheen of seal skin but his lips were powdered with tiny crystals of perspiration.

"Drink this!" Doorne ordered, holding a flask of bush rum to his lips. Tonic swallowed a mouthful and sat up coughing and spitting.

"It hot like fire," he said, opening his mouth wide and gasping.

"Nothing like it to pick you up," Doorne said, taking a swig and passing the flask to Caya and Tengar.

"*This* is bush-rum, father," Caya said appreciatively after he swallowed his drink.

"Is Chinaman the old man does get it from," Tengar said looking sideways at his father. Tonic lay still and shut his eyes but the sun pricked his eyeballs and he turned over on his stomach. The others sat near him with their backs to the sun. Doorne took out a delicately wrought, white clay pipe and used a dry stem of paragrass to clean it.

"We really take long to reach Black Bush this time," Caya said.

"All right, don't make bad worse," Tengar said. Tonic had fallen asleep and was wheezing softly. Saliva was running from

[3]*kinnah*: poison.

9

the corner of his open mouth. The old man struck a match and puffed away at his pipe. In the afternoon sun his head looked like a beach strewn with patches of dirty foam. His face was shaped like an upturned pear – high mongolian cheekbones and hollow cheeks tapering down to a pointed cleft chin. It was lean as a harpy eagle's and the eyes, deep set, were restless. Veins stood out like bush rope at the side of his temples and Tengar could see them throbbing. Ever since he could remember, his father had had those bulging veins at the side of his head. When he was a boy he used to think that the old man had lizards puffing under his skin.

"We better start fixing up camp before a tiger snatch-up one of we tonight," Doorne said.

"Rest you bones, Old Man, long time yet before sundown," Caya said. He sat cross-legged, scratching his naked belly and chewing a black sage stem. His almond-shaped eyes were smoky – oriental eyes set in a Negro's face. Doorne's sons were all by different mothers and Caya's had been a Chinese-Negro mixture.

"Come on, get up!" Doorne ordered and he turned on Caya. "What I forget 'bout this part of the world you en't begin to learn yet. Who is you, Boy, to tell you father 'bout when is time to pitch camp . . . ?"

"All right, Old Man, all right. Stop frying-up you lil fat," Caya said standing up and stretching.

Tonic was rested and refreshed and he went to the edge of the forest to get firewood. The afternoon sun had lost its sting and flocks of birds were flying home after feeding in the swamps or on the seashore. Parrots screamed and chattered in the nearby trees as Tonic hacked at dry branches with his cutlass. A snake with silvery scales slithered past him and he chopped it in two, watching the halves wriggle until his father bellowed at him to hurry up. Tengar and Caya had already driven uprights into the ground and were tying on cross-beams with bush rope.

"Go and bring some troolie palm leaf, Boy, and do it bird-speed!" Caya ordered. Tonic obeyed quickly. He didn't want darkness to catch him too far away from the others. He heard the night wind in the trees and shivered.

Night fell suddenly. The lazy mosquitoes which had been sleeping under the trees all day came out in clouds. The old man and his sons crouched around a fire bathing their limbs in smoke. As soon as a tongue of flame escaped they smothered it with green leaves. Doorne left his sons and sat away from the fire. He heard Tonic alternately coughing from the smoke and slapping mosquitoes.

"You can't control yourself, Boy?" he shouted.

"These mosquitoes stinging like pepper, Papa."

"Damn stupidness!"

"You blood get old and bitter, Old Man, mosquito don't like it no more," Caya said.

"Don't make you eye pass me, Boy," the old man said chuckling.

"They going to let up in a lil while, I can feel the wind clearing up the thickness in the air," Tengar said encouragingly. He inhaled the aromatic smell of wild mango in the wood smoke and remembered how his mother used to burn green limbs inside their hut to kill the stink of dirty bedclothes and sweat.

Dew fell noiselessly and the night wind grew chill. A piper owl sang to the new moon.

"They say them owl is jumbie bird, and nobody never see one," Tonic said hugging his knees tightly.

"I see plenty. They got big eye and they does eat small snake," Tengar said.

"When I was young I try to tame one, jus' to hear he sing when the moon come out, but the one I had never sing a note and he kill so much of the neighbour chicken that me mother drown he in a bucket of water," Doorne said.

They ate tasso[4] and cassava bread[5] for dinner and when Tonic complained that the tasso was like a car tyre, Doorne boasted, "I chewing up this tasso like it is fresh meat," and he added, spitting out a splinter of bone, "all you young boy teeth make out of jelly."

The fire burned steadily and the green logs hissed. In the firelight Doorne's face could have been a burnished mark nailed against the wall of night.

Tengar, Caya and Tonic lay in their hammocks. Tonic had fallen asleep instantly but his brothers watched the stars through holes in the thatch. They heard the piper owl fluting its melodies to the moon, a tinamou singing across the tree tops to its mate, howler baboons roaring and the wind in the bamboo trees. The sounds faded and died in sleep.

A family of red howlers feeding on bamboo shoots woke them

[4]*tasso*: a cheap form of meat.

[5]*cassava bread*: bread made from ground nuts of the cassava bush.

up at day-break. Doorne brought the dying fire to a blaze while his three sons went down to the edge of the swamp to wash. They sat down to a breakfast of turtle eggs, salted fish, biscuits and unleavened bread with bits of pork in it and they washed the meal down with tea.

"I had a funny dream last night," Tonic said, putting a whole turtle egg into his mouth. He always spoke quickly. His mind seemed to push his words out before tongue and lips had time to form them. "I dream that a lot of wolves was calling me."

"Was that tasso sitting heavy on you stomach, Boy," Doorne said, drawing his forearm across his mouth and he added, "We got to get going."

"But that wasn't all the dream," Tonic said.

"Well, tell it quick. We got to go," Doorne said.

"There was an old black man on the other side of the canal and he had teeth like a shark, and every time he talk or sing he teeth was so sharp that they cut his tongue and he mouth was always dripping blood," Tonic said.

"Blood is a good thing to dream 'bout, Boy. It mean that one of we going to make some money," Caya said.

They set out immediately after the meal. There was no washing up as they had used water lily leaves for dishes. Doorne led the way into the twilight of Black Bush. Once out of reach of the sun's rays there was no undergrowth and they moved swiftly, silently across a carpet of rotting leaves. Crouching slightly forward, the old man almost merged with his surroundings. He and Tengar had the hunter's ability of becoming more shadow than substance in the forest. Doorne noticed every movement, even the wind stirring in the leaves high above him. A green parrot snake slid down a mora tree in front of them and when Tonic pointed at it excitedly, his father signalled at him to be quiet. The snake disappeared in the underbush. A bush rabbit stopped in the middle of the trail, standing on its hind legs and examining them with quick darting glances. It sensed no danger. The parrot snake struck so swiftly that the watchers heard a cry and only then noticed that the snake had coiled the rabbit. Doorne whispered to his sons and they walked on quickly until he picked up a bush hog trail. He knelt down and examined the cloven hoofprints carefully.

"They been passing by here couple days well," Doorne whispered. He followed the trail for a little distance, stopped and picked up a section of a snake's backbone.

"Them hog kill a big snake here. That parrot snake better watch out. Once he swallow the rabbit he can't move too far," the old man said in an undertone. He knelt down on the trail again. "This is tiger footmark here, fresh footmark. Is a big puss. He must be following the hog for a meal." His eyes scanned the trees. "Let we climb this one and wait."

Doorne led the way to a big tree with branches spreading over the trail. He wedged his *wareshi* between two branches. The others followed him and they built a rough platform and settled down to wait. Tonic was fidgety but his father and brothers sat alert and still. They were about twenty feet up and above them the tree grew for over a hundred feet boring through the forest ceiling to reach the sunlight. Tonic wormed his way from one end of the platform to the other and Doorne clapped a hand on his bony shoulder.

"Stay quiet!" he hissed. "If you go too near the edge and fall out even Jesus' weeping wouldn't help you."

"I hearing something!" Tengar said and a moment later he pointed down the trail. A jaguar, moving with the ease of a river flowing across a plain, its power hidden under a smooth surface, emerged from the twilight. A marudi bird shouted a raucous warning and there were green fires in the jaguar's eyes as he sniffed suspiciously. He seemed to have picked up their scent. Tonic imagined that the jaguar's eyes and his own were making four all the time. Doorne loaded his fifteen-bore shotgun and waited. Tengar and Caya did not move. They trusted the old man's markmanship.

The thunder of bush hogs coming down the trail broke the silence. The jaguar turned round and sprang on a branch hanging over the trail not far from the watchers.

"We going to have some sport. We got a hunting pardner," Doorne said and some of the tension inside him relaxed as he spoke. His sons laughed mirthlessly, never taking their eyes off the jaguar. The leader of the bush hogs appeared, then the flock, moving in a tightly packed phalanx with the sows and their young ones bringing up the rear. The earth shook with hoofbeats and the forest vibrated with atavistic[6] grunts. Tonic clung to Tengar, the feel of his brother's warm, muscular body was reassuring. The jaguar waited until the main body of hogs had passed by and there were only about a dozen stragglers. He

[6]*atavistic*: primitive.

pounced on a fat sow and buried curved fangs into its neck. There was a piercing squeal cut short by a gurgle. The rest of the flock turned round and stampeded towards the attacker. Sensing danger, the jaguar sprang back on the tree, the hog still gripped in his jaws. The branch broke under the extra weight and the jaguar fell in the midst of the flock. Certain of his strength, he released the dead hog and snarled. The milling, grunting pack closed in on him and he began to force his way through with fangs and claws and fury, maddened by the scent of blood and the pain of his wounds. The hogs that could not reach their enemy turned on the wounded and dying of their own kind and devoured them. Four times it seemed as if the jaguar had cleared enough space around him to spring free, but each time they surged in again. The spot on which he fought became a whirlpool in the middle of a stream of hogs.

"He done kill 'bout twenty of them," Doorne said but the others did not hear him.

The jaguar went down twice more, but he came up and fought back in an impotent frenzy of ebbing strength. He snarled a hoarse admission of defeat and went down for the last time. The hogs played tug-o'-war with his intestines and when nothing was left but blood-stained skin and bones, they remained milling around uncertainly.

Whenever Tonic looked away from the scene of the fight, his eyes fell on the shotgun across Tengar's knees. He had been allowed to use it a few times but Tengar always complained that cartridges were expensive, and that a shotgun was not a small boy's toy.

"Let me take a shot, Tengar," he pleaded but his brother either did not hear him or ignored him. Tonic felt that this was a good chance to bag one or even two of the hogs. He would be a hero at school if he did. He looked at Tengar and then at the gun. He reached for the gun and no one seemed to notice. Grabbing it, he raised the stock to his shoulder and fired quickly. He did not bother to aim or hold the gun close enough. The recoil flung him backwards and before Tengar could reach out to save him, he fell off the platform. The twenty-foot drop dazed him and he sat in the midst of the hogs, nursing a bruised shoulder and showing the lily bulbs of his eyes. The gun lay beside him with one barrel still loaded but he made no attempt to pick it up. The hogs closed in on him and he screamed. Fear gave him strength and cunning. He got up unsteadily and ran towards the base of the tree. If he reached it he could climb up a bush rope. The flock came after him. Tengar sprang down from the platform, a prospecting knife in one hand and a cutlass in the other. Most of the hogs followed Tonic but Tengar stamped his feet and shouted trying to call them away. Tonic, running like a tiger, sprang on to a thick liana, but it had too much slack and he dropped back. He saw the hogs baring their teeth below him and tugged frantically at the vine. Tengar fought the hogs off by crouching low and hacking at their legs. Doorne and Caya sat on the platform, looking on helplessly, the old man fingering the trigger of his gun, and Caya shouting encouragement.

"Hold on, Tonic! Climb up, boy! Don't frighten, Small-boy!"

A big hog caught Tonic by the heel and hauled him down. Tengar had cleared a way to within ten feet of his brother.

"I coming, Tonic, I coming, Boy!" he called out, sweat glistening on his limbs. Tengar's strength was invincible because he was unconscious of it. It was something vibrating in his body like anger or laughter. Many of the hogs had turned away from Tonic and were attacking him now. Every time they rushed at him he swung his cutlass, chopping off forelegs like twigs. Tonic was screaming and foam whitened his lips. Before Tengar reached him, the boy's legs suddenly seemed to melt, he grew shorter and shorter. His screams subsided into a rhythmic moaning. When Tengar cleared a path to his brother, all that was left of the boy's legs were frayed stumps gushing blood and protruding bones with jagged ends. Doorne and Caya joined them. The old man went down on one knee and fired into the flock until the barrel of his gun was too hot to touch. The hogs, their leaders dead, turned and ran. Tonic was lying face down with one eye pressed against a big, star-shaped leaf stained with drops of blood. Ants were scurrying up and down the leaf and before lapsing into unconsciousness, he saw them as huge monsters. Doorne tied a tourniquet around the stumps, cooing to his son all the time like a mother baboon nursing a wounded baby. The sweet and sticky smell of blood and death was everywhere. Caya helped his father to wash Tonic's wounds, but Tengar stood with his back against the tree holding the dripping cutlass in his hand. A sense of community was awakened between Doorne and his sons. He was again the father, the one in authority.

"You got some water in you balata pouch. Give the boy some and wash this froth off his mouth," he ordered and Tengar obeyed mechanically. Caya went around clubbing wounded hogs to death. The ground was slippery with blood. Tengar wet his handkerchief and mopped his brother's face. Tonic opened his eyes and said:

"Tengar, me don't want Mantop[7] to call me yet but I feeling funny. Me head feel like a kite flying over me ..."

"Don't talk so much, Boy. Lie down quiet," Doorne said.

"Is why me foot feelin' so heavy, Papa?"

"You get injure, Boy, bad injure."

"Tengar!"

"Aye, aye, Small-boy."

"Is how you does know when Mantop come for you?"

"You does jus' know, Small-boy. You don't never need no prophet to tell you."

"Is how you does know ... how you does know ... how ... " Tonic's voice trailed off. Tengar and Doorne stood over him crying softly. The skin around the stumps of Tonic's legs was turning yellow.

"You think he got a chance?" Caya asked.

"He loss too much blood," Doorne said. Tonic's breath was coming as if it was retched from his body. Suddenly it stopped and blood poured from his mouth.

"Small-boy! Small-boy!" Tengar called urgently. Tonic's eyes looked like eggs in a dark nest. Caya was calculating how much money the pork would fetch in the village. He did not notice when his brother died. Tengar covered the dead boy's legs with a dirty blanket and stood over the corpse.

"Is why folks we does die so stupid!" he shouted, waving his his arms about, challenging enemies in the forest whom he was sure lurked and listened everywhere. "Is why we folks does die so stupid? In other place, they say, people does die for something. But is why Tonic die, tell me that?"

[7]*Mantop*: the boy's word for God.

The Tallow[1] Pole

Barnabas J. Ramon-Fortune *(Trinidad)*

It was the day of the contest and everything was prepared. From the top of the pole dangled a ham, a bottle of whisky and a bottle of rum, fastened there by short ends of rope, and resting on the very top was a small cardboard box containing a hundred-dollar note.

I stood in the mixed crowd watching the pole that rose twenty to twenty-five clean, straight feet into the air like a ship's mast without rigging, greased from top to base with tallow after it had been planed and sand-papered to the smoothness of glass. The tallow stood on it in blotchy, white lumps like a strange, horrible fungoid disease; but it had begun to melt in the heat and the grease ran down sluggishly like ugly, shapeless drops of sweat from the hide of some prehistoric animal.

Standing at the foot of the pole, a couple of feet away, was the Mayor looking at his watch. He was dressed in a loose, linen suit that sagged about him. He seemed to be personally affected by the heat. He was a tall, massive, black man with a thick moustache that looked like a tangle of black shoelaces. His thick, kinky hair looked rigid and affrighted on his head.

It was Monday morning and you could feel the heat rising like waves below you from the bowels of the earth. It seemed as if the sun had changed its centre and that it no longer burned in the sky but somewhere close to the surface of the ground, waiting for the earth to crack, and leap out, a fearful, unformed foetus of fire. But when you shaded your eyes with your damp, clammy hands and looked up, you knew that *he* was still in his old place in the sky, sneering and relentless, grinning at you with his blazing teeth. The glare was all around you, enveloping you, penetrating the lids of your eyes, shining through your skin, so that as you held up your hand against the sun you could see its huge spider of bones.

At twelve noon the contest would begin. I saw it was two minutes to twelve.

The Mayor puckered his lips as he watched the face of his

[1] *Tallow*: wax.

watch and then shouted:

"Start!"

The first contestant leapt at the pole and immediately slipped to the earth with great speed, striking it violently with his posterior. He wore a pair of old, khaki shorts and a merino.[2] Tallow clung under his armpits, to his chin and all along one side of his face.

The mixed crowd of about four hundred let out a hollering burst of laughter as he picked himself up, an enormous, magnified fly that had just unstuck itself from flypaper.

The Mayor was mopping his brow and laughing while the sweat poured into his eyes.

The other contestant went up to the pole, turned to the crowd and bowed. Then he turned to the pole again. There was a feline[3] quality about him, in his long, thin, nimble limbs, like a tree that had grown too high too quickly. His plan seemed not to attack the pole violently as the last man had done but to woo it like a lover. He made a short leap and held it. For a moment he was stuck there like a fly floundering on water, beating arms and legs furiously without making progress in any direction. Then he slipped gradually to the bottom, striking the ground with his knees and toes, while he embraced the base of the pole like a weeping mother fondling and trying to bring back a dead child to life.

The pole now, at least the lowest ten feet of it, was a clean and shining brown pillar of wood. All the grains of the wood could be clearly seen, like brushmarks in a painting. They flowed white and clean with artistic widenings and narrowings and now and then swelled into circular shapes that flow around a knot. The knots looked like onions embedded in the smooth, clean surface of the wood.

I observed now that the contestants were not slipping quite so easily down the pole. The same men, after cleaning themselves of the clinging grease with pieces of bagging, came back again and again to try their skill. Every now and then a contestant progressed about six inches, bringing down with him generous handfuls of tallow.

Many contestants brought sand and bags to assist them in their climb. Mounds of sand were stacked a few feet away from

[2]*merino*: soft woollen jacket.
[3]*feline*: cat-like.

the pole and the coarse material of sugar and rice bags lay here and there in the small, human arena with the pole standing challengingly in the centre of it like Mount Everest.

Then gradually, but quickly gaining in intensity, there was a stir in the crowd and a rise in the sound of voices over and above the prevailing general hubbub. It echoed from one side of the crowd to the other.

"Greasy Pole! Greasy Pole!"

I had heard about him; everybody had heard about him.

But I had never before had the opportunity of seeing the great Greasy Pole.

The people fell back making a passage for the great man. Greasy Pole had won the contest continuously over the past five years.

The crowd flowed in again, closing ranks, like the return of the waters of the Red Sea after the passage of the Israelites, and Greasy Pole stood in the arena.

He was short, black; blacker than any Negro I had ever seen; true black – and shining; as if his sebaceous glands gave his skin a special glow. His kinky hair on his perfectly round head was cropped short and could only be distinguished from the round shape of his skull by its dusty dullness. He carried a heap of bags over his left shoulder. The span of his shoulders was broad and his arms looked like grappling tentacles where they emerged from his dusty white merino. He wore a pair of khaki shorts roughly patched in the seat, apparently by his own square, thick hands. But it was his feet and his toes that held my attention. They were long, unusually long for his height, with large middle joints that seemed endowed with extraordinary gripping powers. As he walked they gripped and clenched the earth, leaving a deep footprint where he had passed.

He stood before the pole and looked up and down as if measuring an adversary.[4] Not a smile played on his face; his eyes were tense, ignoring the crowd as if he alone stood there. The long line between his thick, black lips was hard, straight and immobile. In the next instant, his broad face became as active as water stirred by the wind, and he smiled. He had discovered the weakness of his adversary. He turned to the crowd for the first time, and bowed.

"Greasy Pole! Greasy Pole!" the cheers went up.

[4]*adversary*: opponent, rival.

He stood erect again but immediately stooped and gathered up some tallow from the ground. He rubbed it over the entire front of his body down to his legs in a thin film. Then he walked over to one of the heaps of sand and, taking up great handfuls, sprinkled himself liberally with it. The front of his body looked like a large sheet of sandpaper.

He walked back to the pole and taking a spring, leapt upon it. He did not slip down. His enormous, claw-like toes spread open to the smooth, circular surface of the pole and bit into it greedily.

The crowd screamed and swayed. Someone behind me thumped me on my back.

Greasy Pole remained there clenched upon the pole for a few seconds, gripping it like a wrestler in a stranglehold. His body jerked and he moved up several inches. Soon his hands reached the line of the tallow where the highest contestant before him had left his mark. I could see the tension in his legs. His toes were like talons. His body jerked again and his hands swept into the tallow.

He began to slip down, slowly but surely. Then he stopped. He seemed stuck to the pole – pinned upon the pole; gripping it with his thighs and looking like a hideous, misshapen, black butterfly.

He remained there, panting. His latissimus dorsi[5] stood out like large wings. He took his hands one after the other from the pole and flung the tallow to the ground.

His body shook again. His great toes, completely spread apart, lifted him up and up again quickly to the high triumphant tallow mark.

He was hurrying now. His hands swept into the tallow greedily, quickly, rapidly, as he flung great lumps of it to the ground.

The crowd screamed again as he neared the top. There seemed no point in his pausing now; no point in his stopping and taking breath; he must get to the top now, or fail.

He passed the ham; he was going for the hundred dollars.

The heat and the excitement held us spellbound. A *cigale*[6] was crying against the hot noon. Except for that, the world seemed to be cast in an eternal silence.

Suddenly, the crowd turned as if someone had fired a shot into the air. Greasy Pole stopped, too.

[5]*latissimus dorsi*: back bones.
[6]*cigale*: cicada, Tropical grasshopper.

Someone was calling the name George Baker. It was a woman's voice.

"George Baker! George Baker!"

She was shouting from the back of the crowd but her voice cut over our heads like a scythe.

Greasy Pole turned and looked over the heads of the crowd to where the voice was coming from.

"George Baker! Don't forget you promise me dat money las' night! De money on top o' de pole is mine! George Baker, you got to mind you chile!"

Greasy Pole's body sagged. His muscles slunk back into the smooth, level surface of his skin.

There was a heavy sigh from four hundred throats as Greasy Pole slipped slowly down the pole and alighted to the ground. He looked at us with a sad, disappointed face as if he had failed us.

In my mind's eye I saw the infant, not yet a year old, with large, black eyes, the paternity of which Greasy Pole was probably disputing. Was it boy or girl? I would never know. It did not matter.

Greasy Pole bowed his head in shame and defeat and walked through the crowd.

Later that evening I passed Greasy Pole. In fact, I stepped over him. He was lying drunk on the pavement.

A Village Tragedy

John Hearne *(Jamaica)*

The old boar slashed Ambrose Beckett across the top of his thigh, almost severed his private parts, and dragged three feet of his gut out on the tip of one tusk. It was done between one brazen squeal and another, while Ambrose Beckett still turned on the wet clay of the path and before the echo of his last, useless shot wandered among the big peaks around the valley.

The men with whom Ambrose Beckett had been hunting turned and saw the ridge-backed, red-bristled beast vanish like a cannon-ball into a long stretch of fairy bamboo. Before they reached him, they saw Ambrose Beckett's wildly unbelieving face, like gray stone beneath the brown, and the dark arches of his spurting blood shining on the wet dull clay under the tree ferns. Then he had fallen like a wet towel among the leaf mould, clutching the clay in his slack fingers, with one distant, protesting scream sounding from the back of his throat.

They bandaged him, after stuffing, inexpertly, bits of their shirts and handkerchiefs into his wounds. Nothing they did, however, could stop a fast, thick welling of blood from where he had been torn. And no comfort could stop his strangled, faraway screaming. They made some sort of stretcher from two green branches and a blanket. They covered him with another blanket and began to carry him across the mountains to the village. The trial was very narrow, and the floor of the rain forest was steep and wet. Each time they slipped and recovered balance they jolted the stretcher. After a while, they forced themselves not to shudder as Ambrose Beckett screamed. Soon he began to moan, and the slow, dirty blood began to trickle from his mouth, and they knew that he would never reach the village alive.

When they realised this, they decided to send Mass' Ken's half-witted son, Joseph, ahead of them to tell the doctor and the parson. Joseph was the biggest idiot any man could remember being born in the village. He inhabited a world of half-articulate fantasy and ridiculous confusion. He was strong enough to kill a man with his hands, and he wept if a child frowned at him. In Cayuna, the children do not, as yet, throw stones at their

22

naturals, but they tease them, and often Joseph, who loved to wait outside the school and watch the children going home, would be seen crouched between the roots of the cotton tree, weeping disconsolately because the boys had scowled as they passed and said, "Joseph! What you doin' here, man?" He could learn nothing, and remembered little from one minute to the next unless you dealt him a blow across the head when giving him the simplest instructions. But he was marvellous on the mountains: tireless as a mule and much faster.

Now, with Ambrose Beckett dying on the blanket, the men standing around gave Joseph his instructions. "Doctor!" said Mass' Ken, his father, and cuffed him across the head. "Doctor! You hear?" He hit him again. "Tell doctor an' tell parson dem mus' come quick. Tell dem come quick, you hear! Tell dem Mass' Ambrose sick bad. Sick! Sick! You hear!" Joseph's big, stone head rocked again under a blow, and his odd, disorganised face closed its askew planes into a grin of pure understanding. He went off among the huge trees and thick wet bush and into the mist. When he had gone ten steps they could no longer hear him.

It was twelve miles and four thousand feet down to the village, and he did it in four hours. At ten o'clock that night he started to bang happily on the door of the manse and kept it up until the Reverend Mackinnon put his head out of the window. When he heard the shutter slamming against the wall, Joseph ran to the middle of the lawn, capering and shouting.

"What?" called the Reverend Mackinnon. "What is it, Joseph?"

He could see nothing but a vague, starlit blur, bounding up and down on the lawn, but he recognised the manner and the voice. Joseph jumped higher and shouted again, his voice tight and brazen with self-importance.

Finally the Reverend Mackinnon came downstairs and cuffed the boy until he became calm. Then he got the story.

"Doctor!" he said, turning Joseph around and giving him a push. Leaving the parson, Joseph ran across the damp Bahama grass of the lawn to where he could see the deep yellow of a light in one window of a big house along the road. Doctor Rushie was still up; it was one of the nights that he got drunk, as he did, regularly and alone, twenty times a month.

"Good God!" said Rushie. "How far up did it happen?"

Joseph gestured. Distance, except in terms of feet and yards, was not of much importance in his life.

23

"Have you told parson?" the doctor asked. He was drunk, but not much. Had the news come a little later he would have been very drunk and quite incapable. He went to the window and bawled for his servant. "Saddle the mule," shouted Doctor Rushie, "and put on your clothes. Bring a lantern. Hurry up!"

In about five minutes the doctor was riding out of the village, with his manservant trotting ahead, the circle of light from the lantern sliding quickly from side to side across the path and making the shadows of the hillside and valley drop deeper. There was a stand of golden-cup trees along this stretch of the bridle path, and the dropped fruit broke wetly under the hoofs of the mule, and a thick, sugary scent came up on the cold air, cutting through the hot, oily smell of the lantern.

They overtook the Reverend Mackinnon, who had no manservant and who was riding his stubby, gray gelding alone in the dark. By the lantern light Doctor Rushie could see the parson's very pale long face and his lank gray hair fallen across his forehead and full of burrs from the long grass of the steep bank beside the narrow path.

"You've heard?" the doctor said. It was not really a question, and they were riding on in the darkness behind the bob and sway of the lantern while the parson was nodding his head.

Back on the road, Joseph sat on a big stone outside the doctor's house. Nobody had told him what to do after delivering his messages, and he felt confused and restless. The doctor's house, and the Reverend Mackinnon's, were up the road from the village. Neither man had thought to inform the people down there as to what had happened on the mountain. Soon Joseph rose from the stone, ran down to the village, and began to race about the street from side to side, talking loudly to himself. It was not long before he had awakened every household within sound of his voice.

"Joseph, you bad boy," screeched Mr Tennant, the schoolmaster. "What are you doing here? At this hour." Joseph flapped a big dirty hand at him excitedly. "Boy, if I bring a switch out to you ..." Mr Tennant said. Joseph shot away down the street like a dog, but he continued to talk very loudly.

Mr Tennant, with a tight, moist smile on his plump lips and carrying a long supplejack cane, came from his house. Joseph bolted for the shoemaker's doorway. Only Elvira, Joseph's smallest sister, could get as much sense from his clogged speech as quickly as Mass' Emmanuel, the shoemaker.

"Joseph," said Mass' Emmanuel, as the natural found refuge in his doorway, "why you not sleepin', eh? What a bad boy. I've a good mind to let teacher flog you."

He put an arm across the boy's trembling shoulders and drew him close.

Joseph told him about Ambrose Beckett, imitating with great vividness the terrible, ripping twitch of the boar's head, writhing enthusiastically on the ground to show what it had been like with Mass' Ambrose. Mass' Emmanuel translated as people began to come from the houses. Then they all looked up to the hill at the other end of the village, to where Ambrose Beckett's house stood. They began to move toward the house.

"Lawd King!" said Miss Vera Brownford. "Fancy Mass' Ambrose! A fine man like dat. Poor Miss Louise!"

She was the centre of the older women of the village as they went up the hill to the house where Ambrose and Louise Beckett had lived for thirty years. Vera Brownford was ninety-eight or maybe a hundred. Perhaps she was much more. Her first grandchild had been born before anyone now alive in the village, and only a few people could still remember her, dimly, in early middle age. Her intimate participation in every birth, death, and wedding was, for the village, an obligatory ritual. She had lived so long and so completely that she had grown to want nothing except freedom from pain. She had even transcended the brief, fierce resurgence of the child's longing for recognition which had assailed her again when she was about seventy. At times the shadow line between life and death was not very distinct to her expectation, her desire, or her feeling, but she understood the terror and confusion that the crossing of the line brought to those younger than herself. And understanding this, she gave comfort as a tree gives shade, or as a stream gives water to those who fetch it, with a vast, experienced impartiality. It was her occupation.

Among the younger men and women Joseph was still the centre of interest as they went up the hill. His mime performance of Ambrose Beckett and the boar had begun to acquire the finish of art. In all his life he had never experienced such respect for his ability and knowledge. He was almost gone out of his poor mind with happiness.

"Joseph," said Mass' Emmanuel suddenly, coming back down the path which was leading them to Louise Beckett's darkened house, "Joseph. I forget. We gwine to need ice fe' pack Mass Ambrose. Tell dem to give you ice. Ice, you hear. At Irish Corner."

He gave a five-shilling note to the boy and hugged the huge, smoothly sloping shoulders and smiled at him. Only for two people, Elvira and Emmanuel, would Joseph remember anything unaccompanied by a blow.

Joseph turned and raced down the path. He seemed to weave through the murmurous crowd like a twist of smoke. Before he was out of earshot they heard him singing his own chant, which was a mingle of all the hymns and songs he had ever listened to. He was always adding to it, and though it had no more conscious structure than a roll of thunder, it had a remarkable pervasive quality, coming to you from a dozen points at once, with odd limping echoes.

The Reverend Mackinnon and Doctor Rushie met the party of returning hunters about five miles from the village. They heard the dogs barking and saw the lantern lights jump along the pines on the saddle between the peaks ahead of them. This was on the side of a great valley, on a trail worn through a stretch of ginger lilies. The night was very cold, and mist was coming down from the sharp, fuzzy peaks and piling into the valley below, and the air was full of a thin spicy tang as the hoofs crushed the long ginger-lily leaves against the stones.

"Ho-yah!" shouted the doctor's manservant when they saw the lights. "Is dat you, Mass' Ken?"

"Yes." The answer rolled back slowly, thin and lost in the air of the huge valley. "Who dere?"

"Doctor. Doctor and parson. How Mass' Ambrose stay?"

"Him dead!"

He was dead, right enough, when the two parties met. In the glare from the lanterns his skin was the colour of dough and earth mixed, quite drained of blood. The blankets between which he lay were dark and odorous with his blood. His mouth had half opened, and one eye had closed tightly, twisting his face and leaving the other eye open. It gave him an unbelievably knowing and cynical leer.

"Well, I'll be damned," Doctor Rushie said, and then, seeing Mackinnon's face, "Beg your pardon; but look at that."

"Look at what?" the Reverend Mackinnon said stiffly. He had never liked Rushie much, and now he did not like him at all.

"His face. How many dead men have you seen?"

"I don't know. As many as you I suppose."

"Exactly," Doctor Rushie said. "Probably more. But how many have you seen die with one eye closed? You know, it's generally both eyes wide open. Sometimes both closed, but not often. Damned odd, eh?"

"I hardly think it's important, doctor," the Reverend Mackinnon said. His long, ugly, Scots face was tightly ridged with disgust. Only the presence of the villagers kept him polite.

"No," the doctor said, "it's not important. I just noticed it. Well, no point hanging around here. Let's get him home, eh?"

Going down the track, the doctor and the parson rode behind.

"What a dreadful thing to have happened, eh, doctor?" said the Reverend Mackinnon. "I can hardly believe it."

He always felt guilty about not liking Doctor Rushie; and he constantly asked himself wherein he as a minister had failed to contact the drunken, savagely isolated creature who rode behind him.

"I can believe it," the doctor said. "Do you know how many ways the world has of killing you? I was adding up the other night. It comes to thousands. Simply thousands."

The Reverend Mackinnon could find no answer to this. There were answers, he knew, but none that he cared to risk with the lonely, brutal man who, more or less, cared for the health of their village and a score of other villages in the district.

He's not even a very good doctor, the Reverend Mackinnon thought, and felt a cold flush of shame because the thought gave him satisfaction.

"He was such a strong, vital man, too," the Reverend Mackinnon said a little later. He was unable to bear the night with the mist blowing damp and cold across his face, and the bobbing lanterns lighting up the silent men as they scrambled awkwardly with the stretcher on the narrow track.

"He was a strong man," the doctor said dryly.

"Why, the other day I saw him clearing that land of his up by the river, with his sons. He was doing twice as much as they," Mackinnon continued.

"Oh, he was a good farmer, all right," the doctor agreed, in the same dry tone. "He ought to have been, with what he had acquired these last few years. He knew what he wanted, all right."

"He was an example to his community," Mackinnon said with

solemn emphasis. "God-fearing and responsible. An example. If only he had had an education. They would have made him a justice of the peace. He was an example. A Christian example."

"Well, maybe the boys will become examples, too," the doctor told him.

"The boys," said the Reverend Mackinnon, "the boys have fallen far from the stem. Thomas has his father's sense of duty, but he is weak. Weak. And Sidney cares only for himself, his pleasures, and his land. He caused Ambrose Beckett a great deal of worry. Which one of them do you think will get the holding, eh? Thomas or Sidney?"

"Couldn't say," the doctor replied. "I was only Beckett's doctor, not his lawyer. Probably they'll have equal shares. He had enough, God knows, for these parts."

The Reverend Mackinnon frowned and shifted uneasily in the saddle. Oh, God, he said to himself, make Thomas get the holding. He looked sombrely over the nodding head of his beast and at the vague blur of the stretcher. The men were moving fast now, because Ambrose Beckett was dead and they could heave the stretcher about quickly.

Twenty years before this, Ambrose Beckett had rented land from the church. It was the first move in a programme which had made him the largest peasant farmer in the parish. It had been good land, and he had paid a good rent. But since the war, when everything had gone up, the rent had fallen to a fraction of the land's value, and the Reverend Mackinnon had been looking for some way to increase it. He was, essentially, a timid man, who felt courage and confidence only on Sunday, when he stood unassailable in the pulpit, beyond interruption, with God and the Hosts at his back.

His method of attack in the matter of the rent had been to mount a series of hints. Veiled and offhand at first, they had evolved, after three years, into frequent references about the difficulties and embarrassments of a priest in the modern world. Pride and timidity had kept him from stating an open claim. These and the reasonable certainty that Ambrose Beckett would, at first, refuse to pay more. Would refuse with the plausibility and righteousness of a man who valued an acre, really, more than he regarded a wife and who knew his own usefulness as a parishioner.

I am not covetous, the Reverend Mackinnon told himself in the darkness. I do not want it for myself. But the manse is falling to bits, and if I send Jean home next year she will need clothes. Perhaps two sets within the year; girls grow so fast at her age.

Given time, he knew, he could have persuaded Ambrose Beckett. It would have been painful, but it would have come. Now he would have to begin again with the sons. If Thomas were the heir, it would be easy. He was a gentle, almost girlish lad, very devout and proud of his family's influence in the church. But Sidney. Sidney would be difficult. Difficult and slow. And arrogant. He had always treated the Reverend Mackinnon with a casual politeness more infuriating than hostility. A bland indifference which only on occasion became genially ferocious. The afternoon, for instance, when Mackinnon had caught him making love to a little East Indian girl under a huge rock by the river. The lad had raised his head from beside the girl's blind, contorted face and stared at the parson with cool amused malice. And the next day, Sunday, while Mackinnon was preaching a sermon on the sin of fornication, he had looked down from the pulpit to the front pew where Ambrose Beckett sat in a hot, high-buttoned black suit among his family and seen such a sparkle of conspiratorial intimacy in Sidney's eyes that he had floundered in his speech.

While they were bringing the body of Ambrose Beckett down from the mountain, Joseph had reached the market town of Irish Corner. He knocked on the zinc fence around the shop until the Chinese keeper came down and a small crowd gathered. Then he told the story of Ambrose and the boar again, giving a really practised and gigantic performance. He had great difficulty in making them understand what had happened, or what he wanted, but they finally got it. Then they cut a great block of ice, wrapped it in a crocus bag, hoisted it on to his head, and set him on the road back to the village.

He had hardly stopped running since the late afternoon, and he streamed with sweat as if he had been put under a hose; but he was not tired and he was crazy with excitement. He had never played such a central part in anything before.

Suddenly he slowed his long, effortless jog trot up the steep road. He stopped. The ice in its wrapping of crocus bag was cool and wet between his hands and on his huge, idol's head. From his great, heaving lungs there burst an ecstatic grunt. Ice ... ice ... *ice*. If he got back quickly, they would chip a white, glittering, jagged lump for him. A piece with a point around which he could curl his tongue. A bit to hold above his opened mouth, so that the cold, unimaginable drops would hit the back of his throat. A bit with edges he could rub across tightly shut eyelids and then feel the cold water drying on his skin. He danced with happiness, balancing the huge block as if it were a hat. As far up as his village, ice was still a luxury for all but the doctor, who had a machine which made ice cubes.

The people at Ambrose Beckett's house heard the dogs as the men came up the hill. Louise Beckett rushed from the house and down the path toward the light from the lanterns. When she saw the stretcher she began to cry and moan wildly, covering her face and clutching her body. Her two sons came close to her.

"Mother . . . Mother," Thomas said. He embraced her tightly and began to cry too.

Sidney put his arm around her shoulder and said softly: "I will take care of you, Mother. I will take care of you. Don't cry. Don't cry."

Inside the house, the body was laid out on the kitchen table. The table was too short, and the feet hung over the edge. Doctor Rushie shut the people out and by the light of four lamps sewed up the hideous openings in Ambrose Beckett's body. Once during this operation he spoke, as if to the corpse. "You poor devil," he said, "this must have hurt like blazes. But the other thing would have hurt you more, and it would have lasted longer."

Outside, in the tiny stiffly furnished drawing room, Vera Brownford sat on the old-fashioned horsehair sofa. Louise Beckett sat close up beside her, resting her head on that old, indestructible breast which, thin and hard as a piece of hose pipe, was yet as hugely comfortable as a warm ocean.

"Cry good, child," Vera Brownford said. "Cry good. If you don't cry you will get sick. Oh, Lawd, it hard to lose a man. It hard to lose a good man like Ambrose. Cry good, child. It much easier."

The old, dry voice flowed smoothly, uttering banalities that sheer experience gave the weight of poetry. Louise Beckett cried noisily.

The women of the village stood around the sofa; the men gathered near the door and outside, each group around one of the hunters, who told in whispers what it had been like. The children waited on the fringes of each group; some of them looked with wide stares toward the locked kitchen door.

The Reverend Mackinnon hovered between the men and the

women. Finally he went across to Louise Beckett. "Louise," he said, "you must take comfort. Remember your beloved husband is not gone. He only waits for you in our Master's house. He was a good man, Louise. A true Christian man. Take comfort in that and in the promise of everlasting life."

Louise Beckett raised her stunned face and looked at him from red eyes. "Thank you, parson," she whispered, and burrowed her head against Vera Brownford's breast.

Among the men, Sidney was saying in a hard unbelieving voice: "Jesus, it happen so quick. I tell you, Mass' Emmanuel, it happen before we even see it."

"How things happen so, eh?" Emmanuel said. "Truly, it is like the Bible say: in the midst of life we are in death."

"That is true, Emmanuel," said the Reverend Mackinnon, joining them. "That is very true." He laid a hand on Sidney's shoulder and gave it a little squeeze. "But remember, as Christians we need not fear death if we live so that death finds us prepared for God. We must remember the life God showed us through His only son, and, in our turn, live so that each day we can say to ourselves: Today I did God's will."

He looked closely at Sidney as he spoke, but the young man's face was closed, sullen with grief, unreadable.

Mr Tennant, the schoolmaster, cleared his throat. He thought very highly of the Reverend Mackinnon, but he also felt that, in the village, he should reinforce the parson. Provide the practical epilogues to the more refined utterance of the church.

"It is you and Thomas now, Sidney," Mr Tennant said. "You must act like men. Work the land as diligently as your father. Look after your good mother . . ."

They heard a hard, heavy grunting outside in the dark, and then Joseph stepped into the room. He was lathered about the lips, with sweat and water from the ice mingled on his face and staining his clothes. Everyone stopped talking when they saw the ice.

Mass' Ken, Joseph's father, took the boy by the arm and led him into the bedroom. Four of the men who had hunted that day with Ambrose Beckett followed him. They stripped the clothes and mattress from the springs and spread old newspapers under the bed. They unwrapped the coarse, shaggy crocus from the ice, and one of the men split it into five great lumps with an ice pick. Then they spread old newspapers on the bare springs and waited awkwardly in the half-dark of the little bedroom where

Ambrose Beckett had lain with his wife for thirty years.

Outside, one of the younger men who had been on the hunt laid his hand shyly on Sidney's arm. "Sidney," he said, "I sorry, you see. If it was me own Papa I couldn't sorry more. Lord, Sidney, don't worry. I will help you. You gwine to need anoder man fe' help you wid dat lan' you an' Mass' Ambrose was clearing. What you gwine to put in it, bwoy? It is one nice piece of ground."

Tears shone in Sidney's eyes. He was remembering how powerful and comforting his father had looked in the sunlight as they cleared the land by the river. His friend's words were sweet and warm and made him feel comforted again.

"T'ank you, Zack," he said, "t'ank you. Thomas an' me will need a help. Papa did want to put citrus in dat piece. Dat is de crop pay well now, you know. Since de war over, everybody want orange oil again."

Thomas looked suddenly and with disturbance at his brother.

"When Papa say we was gwine put citrus in?" he asked. "You know we only talk about it. Las' time we talk, you remember I say we should plant ginger. I like ginger. It safe."

"Everybody plant ginger, Thomas," Sidney said gently and inflexibly. "Papa did always say too much ginger was gwine to kill de small holders. Time some of us plant somet'ing else."

The door to the kitchen opened, and they saw Doctor Rushie framed in the opening, with the lamplight yellow behind him. Sidney and Thomas, Mass' Ken and Emmanuel went into the kitchen and brought the body out. Some of the women began to wail. Louise Beckett set up a long howling cry and ran across the room. She held the dead face between her hands. She was twitching like an exhausted animal.

"Mass' Ambrose," she cried, "Mass' Ambrose."

After they had packed the body among the ice lumps, the Reverend Mackinnon led them in prayer around the bed. Then the people started to go home. All went except Vera Brownford and three of Louise Beckett's closest friends, who stayed to watch the body.

It was now the blackest part of the morning, before the sun began to touch the mountaintops and make the sky glow with pink and green.

The Reverend Mackinnon went home and tiredly unsaddled his stumpy gray gelding. He went up to bed and thought about the gentle, exhausted wife he had buried two years before, and worried about the plump, soundly sleeping daughter a hundred miles away in boarding school.

Doctor Rushie went home, and his manservant led the mule away while the doctor sat down to finish the bottle he had been drinking when Joseph came. He thought about the wounds in Ambrose Beckett's body and whether, if he had got to him right away, he could have saved a life. He thought, also, about the sliver from Ambrose Beckett's rectum which he had sent down to Queenshaven for analysis a week ago and which, he was sure, showed the beginnings of cancer.

Lying in the bed they had shared from childhood, Sidney and Thomas clung to each other and sobbed in the painful, tearing manner of grown men. In between grieving for their father they argued fiercely and quietly as to the wisdom of planting citrus or ginger.

In the room with the body, the women sat and watched. Once Louise Beckett leaned forward and touched the damp sheet wonderingly.

"Mass' Ambrose?" she asked softly. "You gawn? You really gawn?"

In the kitchen of his home, Joseph snuggled into bed beside Elvira, his little sister, and began to cry bitterly. She woke when she heard him crying and asked him what was the matter. He told her how he had run all the way to Irish Corner, and back, with the ice, and of how no one had thought to give him a little piece. The ingratitude and thoughtlessness of the mourners shocked the little girl profoundly. She wiped the tears from his big, sweaty face and hugged him, rocking him in her thin arms and kissing him with little quick maternal pecks.

Very soon he was fast asleep.

The Red Ball

Ismith Khan *(Trinidad)*

"Aye ... Thinny Boney! You want to play?"

One of the boys called out to him, and although he had heard
and knew that they were calling him, he kept pulling out the red
petals of the hibiscus flower, tore off their bottom ends and blew
into the fine pores of needle holes at the base until the petals
swelled out into a thin balloon of pink skin which he pierced with
the straight pin which kept his shirt front closed.

"Match-stick foot! You playin' deaf. You want to play or
don't you want to play?"

In his childish way, the boy had understood that if he answered
to any of the names they coined for him, he would have to live
with it forever. For two weeks now, since they moved to Port of
Spain he had been coming to Woodford Square[1] in the evenings.
At first he sat in the fountain with his thin long legs dangling in
the water, the spray falling on his face, and when no one was
going past he waded across the waist-high water to the green and
mossy man-sized busts where there was the giant of a man
standing lordly amid four half-fish half-woman creatures, a tall
trident in his massive arm pointing to the shell of blue sky.
He had touched the strong green veins running down the calves
of the man's leg with fear, half expecting the severe lips to smile,
or even curl in anger at him, but the lips stood still in their
severity. He then held his cheek close to the small breast of one of
the smiling women seated back to back at the feet of the standing
man, and she seemed to smile. That was the first time he felt as
though he were back in Tunapuna, before they moved.

"Aye you! What you name? You have a name or you ain't
have a name?"

He looked at the boys through slitted eyes, still seated on the
foot-high cement runner that ran around Woodford Square with
tall iron rails pierced deep into the runner. On previous evenings,
when the city workers were still wending their ways home through

[1] *Woodford Square*: A popular square in Port of Spain, the capital of Trinidad;
a haunt for "park orators", unemployed men and passers-by.

the short-cut square, he had stayed away from its centre and its fountain, catching flowers of the yellow and purple *poui* as they spun sailing earthward. He waited like a small animal scenting the wind with his nostrils until some small gust unhinged a flower and he went racing below the path it was slowly tracing as it came spinning and dancing slowly down to earth. During the past week he came and sat on the runner where the boys played cricket until the fireflies came out in the square and the boys went home with their bats and wickets and balls, then he got up and caught some fireflies and put them in a small white phial to put under his pillow so that he could watch them glow when they blew out the kerosene lamp.

"Aye – no name – what is your name?"

"I name Bolan," he said sullenly as he eyed the six or seven boys who had stopped their game and stood about from their batting or bowling or fielding positions waiting on him.

"Well ... you want to play or you don't want to play? Cat bite your tongue or what?"

His parents had left their *ajoupa* hut in Tunapuna and loaned out the two cows to his uncle so that his father could work as a cutlassman on the air bases the Americans were building in Chagauramas and the boy went to "Market School" in the back of the Eastern Market with its thousands of voices of buyers, vendors and live animals screaming through the windows of the school so that he could not hear what the teacher was saying sometimes. That cost six lashes in the palms for what the teacher called "daydreaming". And when he finally understood what was meant by daydreaming he could not help but feel that the teacher had pierced deep into him and discovered a secret he kept from everyone else. Because his mind did, indeed, run away to the smells and sounds of Tunapuna, that the crowing of a chicken in the Eastern Market stimulated. And he came to the square in the evenings because it had in some way seemed like the only place in the city of Port of Spain where people were not chasing him down. It was quiet in the Woodford Square, a strange brooding quiet, not of loneliness or nothingness, but of someone having been there long long ago who had left an insignificant footstep on the landscape. For that was Woodford Square, and the Trinity Church beyond, and the Red House and the Public Library, footsteps left behind by unknown people called British and Spaniards who had gone back to their homes to bury their bones a long, long time ago leaving Woodford Square behind for him, this Tunapuna boy from the sugar cane fields, to come and spend the evenings in.

He still sat on the runner, his long-boned hands hung down between his knees, admitting to himself that the cricket set the boys had was good, three wickets made from sawed off broomsticks, which they had nailed into the ground, two bats, one made from a coconut branch, the other a real store bat that smelled of linseed oil, and a cork ball that had red paint on its surface. He rose, took up the ball, and began hefting it, tossing it up in the air, then catching it to feel its weight, while the other boys looked on in silence.

In Tunapuna he had played with used tennis balls which rich people sold for six cents apiece after they had lost their bounce and elasticity. Only on Sunday matches had he seen a real cork ball and the touch of this one, its rough texture between his fingers, its very colour, gave him a feeling of power. He knew that he could bowl them all down for "duck" with this ball.

The boys first looked at each other questioningly, then they began moving to their playing positions as they watched the thin boy count off fifteen paces. He turned and his feet slapped at the turf moving him along like a feather, his thin long body arched like a bow, the ball swung high in the air, his wrist turned in, and he delivered the shooting red ball that turned pink as it raced to the batsman. The batsman swiped blindly and missed, his head swung back quickly to see how the ball could have gone past him so quickly. "Aye, I aye," the wicket-keeper cried out, as the ball smacked into his hands making them red hot. The fielders who were scattered far off moved in closer to see if they could catch the secret in his bowling, but each time he sent the ball shooting through the air, they missed some small flick of his wrist that made him bowl them all down before they could see the ball.

"You want to come back and play tomorrow?" they asked as they stood about the corner of Frederick and Prince streets, eating black pudding and souse from a vendor who had a charcoal brazier going on the street corner.

The boy jerked his shoulders up and down in an indefinite gesture as he watched the other boys buy an inch, two inches, three inches of the black blood sausages, sizzling in a large tray on the pale red embers.

"How much _you_ want?" the vendor asked, as he stood staring at the heap of hot pink ash in the mouth of the brazier, his thumbs hooked in his pants waist. And again he jerked his shoulders up and down in the same indefinite gesture, and when he thought that the vendor was about to offer him a piece of black pudding for nothing, he moved to the back of the clique of boys and disappeared before the fat old woman turned around to look for him again.

It was turning that salmon and orange light of the evening when the sun's rays and the shadows of the trees in Woodford Square were playing tug-of-war, both stretched out thin in the evening as they pulled upon each other until that singular moment when no one was looking, and night fell upon the ground like a ball of silk cotton descending through the air with its infinite fall until it touched the grass and settled there as if to remain forever. He turned into their long tunnelled gateway on Frederick Street and walked to the far end of the deep backyard, for theirs was the last barrack room close to a high wall that separated the yard in the next street.

As he entered the room he smelled cooking, the smoke of kerosene lamps, fresh-cut grass from his father's clothes, and the faint odour of cigarettes and rum that his father's body exuded.

"Boy, where you does go whole evening instead of stop home here and help your moomah?" his father asked. The boy saw him only late in the evenings now, and each evening he brought home a nip of Black Cat rum. At first the boy thought that they were rich as they said they would become when they left Tunapuna where a nip of rum meant that it was a holiday or a celebration and there was laughter all around.

"Nowhere," he answered, as he hid his phial of fireflies under the straw mat on which he slept.

"No-way No-way ... You beginning to play big shot! You could talk better than your moomah and poopah. Boy! You don't know how lucky you is to be goin' to school. When I was your age ...." His father left the sentence incompleted as he put the nip to his mouth and gargled the rum as though he were rinsing out his mouth then swallowed it.

"Leave the child alone! If that is the way they teach him to talk in school that is the right way," his mother put in in his defence.

"Yes ... but No-way is a place? Show me where No-way is, show me! ... You or he, where No-way is, where this boy does go and idle away he time. You know where he does go?" his father shouted, and then it was one of those moments when he felt as if he had held his mother in front of him as a sort of shield to save himself from a rain of blows.

37

His father then fell into one of those silences. He looked like an old man. He let his hair grow on his head and face unless they were going to Tunapuna. Then he would get a shave and a trim, and tell everyone that he was making three dollars a day at the American base.

His mother meantime moved about in a series of quick motions that came as she was close to finishing up her cooking for the evening. She seemed to get a sudden burst of energy toward the climax that would make the whole evening's preparation of dinner come to an end with a soft breath of finality.

"The man for the room rent come and he say that next week the price´ goin' up by two shillings," she said, as if she were speaking to herself. They lived in one of a long line of barracks that you entered after passing through one of those deep dark gateways on Frederick Street. Inside the yard was a stone "bleach" made up of large boulders whitened by the drying of soap as clothes were spread out in the sun to bleach on the hot stones. There was a yellow brass pipe in the centre of the yard tied to a wooden spike driven in the ground.

"It look as if everything goin' up since *we* come to live in town. Is always the same damn thing. Soon as you have a shilling save . . . two shillings expense come up. As soon as we did have a li'l money save we have to go and get a . . ."

"A child?" his mother asked.

The boy's eyelids jerked up and his eyes met his mother's and he saw her look back quickly into the brazier.

The same feeling flooded across his heart as it had in those days he sat on the runner of the square, waiting for something he could not describe. As he left the square that evening he had felt suddenly released from it, now it was upon him again, clinging to his eyebrows and eyelashes like those invisible cobwebs that hang from trees in the square in the early darkness of the evening.

"Boy, why you don't go and sleep instead of listening to big-people talk?" his father said, and the boy started to get up from the low stool on which he sat.

"He ain't eat yet," the boy's mother said. "At least left him eat. What you want the child to do? Go out in the road so he can't hear what you sayin'? It only have one room and the child have ears just like anybody else. Now come and eat too, before you drink any more."

The boy felt more and more that there were things which he had not noticed about his father before. The way he let a long silence linger between the moment he was spoken to, and his reply. And during a lapse like this, he would press his jaw teeth together and make a terrible grimace, then swallow hard before he spoke again.

"Befo' I drink anymo'! Huh! It ain't *have* no mo' to drink," his father said as he turned the small green bottle upside down, from which two or three drops of amber liquor fell on his protruding tongue.

They had finished eating their dinner in silence when his father said, "Boy, go and full this cup with water." The boy unwound his thin legs from his squatting position and hurried out to the pipe in the yard. He returned and handed it to his father.

"All right, boy . . . go ahead and sleep now."

As he started over to the mat in the corner of the room where he slept, his mother said, "*Boy* this . . . *boy* that! What come over you at all? The child have a name, and it look as if you even forget that too."

His father let his body slowly fall backward and when he was flat on the floor, he stretched his limbs with a sigh of relief and tiredness. His eyeballs were dancing in a frenzy under his closed eyelids, then he spoke after a short silence.

"I too tired to argue with you . . . you hear, woman. I goin' to sleep, so I could go and do the white people work tomorrow, please God."

She turned the lamp down low and went out into the yard to wash the iron pots and enamel plates, and when she returned the boy could hear her talking out loud to herself as she often did these days, yet talking unmistakably to his father, as though she were trying to cloud over what she was saying in a kind of slant by not speaking to him directly.

"Is true," she mumbled, "that we ain't save much, that you believe you work hard for nothing, but don't forget how much we had to borrow to move to Port of Spain. One day when we pay back everybody we will be able to save something. . . ."

From the darkness he heard his father, whom he thought was sound asleep ask her, "And how much we have save in the can?"

She took out the Capstan tin in which she kept the money, and counted out all the coins which they had saved above all their expenses since they had come to the city.

"It have eight shillings save up in the can," she said, in a tone of voice which the boy felt was a disappointed one, as if she too felt that there should be more in the cigarette tin. His father let out only a small noise, and as though he had dreamed the little incident, he went back to sleep again.

The following evening the boy went to Woodford Square again. He was a little late, for he had gone down to the foot of Frederick Street on an errand, and when he entered the square, he saw the boys sitting on the grass, the wickets nailed in the ground in readiness, the bats leaning up against a berry tree, and the ball at their sides. Someone caught sight of him and shouted to the others, "Look Bolan!" and the boys all stood up now. He began running toward them, filled with an excitement such as he had never felt before.

"We was waitin' for you, man ... what make you come so late today?" The boy was pleased beyond words that they had not started the game without him. He squeezed out a shiny red cork ball, brand new, from his pocket with a wide smile on his face such as they had never seen before. They all ran to their places and they played cricket until it was dark in the square. The boy was to be their star bowler from now. At the vendor's stand afterward he paid for all the black puddin' they could eat.

"Gimmie a two-inch piece," someone would call out, and the boy foraged in his pocket, fingering the surface of the red ball each time he reached for a coin to pay the vendor. Along the emptiness of Frederick Street they heard someone calling. The boys looked in turns to see if it might be any of their parents, then fell back to their black puddin'.

Suddenly the boy recognized his father in the cut-away trousers that came three-quarters of the way down his legs. "I have to go," he said hastily, and he ran up Frederick Street. As they turned into the gateway, his father took hold of his ear and tugged him close. "I goin' to give you a cut-ass that you go remember so long as you live," he said, as he led the boy to the back of the yard where an old carpenter had left hundreds of switches of sawed off wood. The boy danced up and down as the lashes rained now on his feet, now on his back. His father shouted at him, "It ain't have no thief in my family ... we never rob nobody a black cent." The boy's mother hovered above, trying to catch the switch from his hand, and each time she caught it he took another from the large pile that lay about on the ground.

"All right," his mother said. "Nobody ain't say that your family rob anybody ... why you don't leave the boy alone?" For each statement of defence from his mother, the boy got more stinging lashes on his legs.

"And where this boy learn to thief from . . . where? Where he learnin' these *bad bad* habits from . . . not from me!" his father said.

"Don't call the child a thief . . . he is not a thief, he just take the money to buy something."

"He is a thief . . . thief," his father insisted, and the switch whistled with each word.

"When I get through with him he never thief in he whole life again, he go remember what it mean to be a thief." The boy's legs were marked with thin red welts from the lashes and he stopped jumping up and down from the switches now. His father, too, seemed tired, and now his mother took hold of the switch in his hand.

"You ain't have no feelin's . . . you done gone and kill the half of this boy that is your half, now leave the half that make out of my body, if you still have any feelin's for that."

She took the boy to the stand pipe and mixed some salt in a cup of water and made him drink it down, then she took out the ball from his pocket and the few pennies of change he had left. She had gone to the square several days looking for the boy and saw him sitting on the runner watching the other boys play, and she had gone away. When she saw the ball, she knew that they had finally asked him to play.

"You still remember how to bowl?" she asked him, and the boy nodded, his eyes fastened to the ground. After they blew out the kerosene lamp the boy rolled from one side of the mat to the other, trying to find a position in which his body would not be painful. He heard his mother talking to his father in whispers, and he was afraid that another argument and another beating would follow. He stopped his ears so that he would not hear their conversation, and long afterwards, when he had fallen asleep with his arms around his head, he dreamed that the great green man standing in the cauldron of water in Woodford Square had moved his lips and spoken to him saying, "I didn't know, boy . . . is for you that we doin' all this . . . only you. We love you like nothin' else in the whole whole world . . . must always remember that."

And when they were all awake in the morning and he wondered if he had dreamed the words that still sang in his ears, he remembered that he had smelled his father's body as he came and lay close to him in the night.

Blackout

Roger Mais *(Jamaica)*

The city was in partial blackout; the street lights had not been turned on, because of the wartime policy of conserving electricity; and the houses behind their discreet *aurelia* hedges were wrapped in an atmosphere of exclusive respectability.

The young woman waiting at the bus stop was not in the least nervous, in spite of the wave of panic that had been sweeping the city about bands of hooligans roaming the streets after dark and assaulting unprotected women. She was a sensible young woman to begin with, who realised that one good scream would be sufficient to bring a score of respectable suburban householders running to her assistance. On the other hand she was an American, and fully conscious of the tradition of American young women that they don't scare easily.

Even that slinking black shadow that seemed to be materializing out of the darkness at the other side of the street did not disconcert her. She was only slightly curious now that she observed that the shadow was approaching her, slowly.

It was a young man dressed in conventional shirt and pants, and wearing a pair of canvas shoes. That was what lent the suggestion of slinking to his movements, because he went along noiselessly – that, and the mere suggestion of a stoop. He was very tall. There was a curious look of hunger and unrest about his eyes. But the thing that struck her immediately was the fact that he was Black; the other particulars scarcely made any impression at all in comparison. In her country not every night a white woman could be nonchalantly approached by a Black man. There was enough novelty in all this to intrigue her. She seemed to remember that any sort of adventure might be experienced in one of these tropical islands of the West Indies.

"Could you give me a light, lady?" the man said.

It is true she was smoking, but she had only just lit this one from the stub of the cigarette she had thrown away. The fact was she had no matches. Would he believe her, she wondered? "I am sorry. I haven't got a match."

The young man looked into her face, seemed to hesitate an

42

instant and said, his brow slightly wrinkled in perplexity: "But you are smoking."

There was no argument against that. Still, she was not particular about giving him a light from the cigarette she was smoking. It may be stupid, but there was a suggestion of intimacy about such an act, simple as it was, that, call it what you may, she could not accept just like that.

There was a moment's hesitation on her part now, during which time the man's steady gaze never left her face. There was pride and challenge in his look, curiously mingled with quiet amusement.

She held out her cigarette towards him between two fingers.

"Here," she said, "you can light from that."

In the act of bending his head to accept the proffered light, he came quite close to her. He did not seem to understand that she meant him to take the lighted cigarette from her hand. He just bent over her hand to light his.

Presently he straightened up, inhaled a deep lungful of soothing smoke and exhaled again with satisfaction. She saw then that he was smoking the half of a cigarette, which had been clinched and saved for future consumption.

"Thank you," said the man, politely; and was in the act of moving off when he noticed that instead of returning her cigarette to her lips she had casually, unthinkingly flicked it away. He observed this in the split part of a second that it took him to say those two words. It was almost a whole cigarette she had thrown away. She had been smoking it with evident enjoyment a moment before.

He stood there looking at her, with cold speculation.

In a way it unnerved her. Not that she was frightened. He seemed quite decent in his own way, and harmless; but he made her feel uncomfortable. If he had said something rude she would have preferred it. It would have been no more than she would have expected of him. But instead, this quiet contemptuous look. Yes, that was it. The thing began to take on definition in her mind. How dare he; the insolence!

"Well, what are you waiting for?" she said, because she felt she had to break the tension somehow.

"I am sorry I made you waste a whole cigarette," he said.

She laughed a little nervously. "It's nothing," she said, feeling a fool.

"There's plenty more where that came from, eh?" he asked.

"I suppose so."

This won't do, she thought, quickly. She had no intention of standing at a street corner jawing with – well, with a Black man. There was something indecent about it. Why doesn't he move on? As though he had read her thoughts he said:

"This is the street, lady. It's public."

Well, anyway, she didn't have to answer him. She could snub him quietly, the way she should have properly done from the start.

"It's a good thing you're a woman," he said.

"And if I were a man?"

"As man to man maybe I'd give you something to think about," he said, still in that quiet, even voice.

In America they lynch them for less than this, she thought.

"This isn't America," he said. "I can see you are an American. In this country there are only men and women. You'll learn about it." She could only humour him. Find out what his ideas were about this question, anyway. It would be something to talk about back home. Suddenly she was intrigued.

"So in this country there are only men and women, eh?"

"That's right. So to speak there is only you an' me, only there are hundreds and thousands of us. We seem to get along somehow without lynchings and burnings and all that."

"Do you really think that all men are created equal?"

"It don't seem to me there is any sense in that. The facts show it ain't so. Look at you an' me, for instance. But that isn't to say you're not a woman, the same way as I am a man. You see what I mean?"

"I can't say I do."

"You will, though, if you stop here long enough."

She threw a quick glance in his direction.

The man laughed.

"I don't mean what you're thinking," he said. "You're not my type of woman. You don't have anything to fear under that heading."

"Oh!"

"You're waiting for the bus, I take it. Well, that's it coming now. Thanks for the light."

"Don't mention it," she said, with a nervous sort of giggle.

He made no attempt to move along as the bus came up. He stood there quietly aloof, as though in the consciousness of a male strength and pride that was justly his. There was something about him that was at once challenging and disturbing. He had shaken her supreme confidence in some important sense.

As the bus moved off she was conscious of his eyes' quiet scrutiny, without the interruption of artificial barriers, in the sense of dispassionate appraisement, as between man and woman, any man, any woman.

She fought resolutely against the very natural desire to turn her head and take a last look at him. Perhaps she was thinking about what the people on the bus might think. And perhaps it was just as well that she did not see him bend forward with swift hungry movement, retrieving from the gutter the half-smoked cigarette she had thrown away.

The Enemy

V.S. Naipaul *(Trinidad)*

I had always considered this woman, my mother, as the enemy.
She was sure to misunderstand anything I did, and the time came
when I thought she not only misunderstood me, but quite
definitely disapproved of me. I was an only child, but for her
I was one too many.

She hated my father, and even after he died she continued to
hate him.

She would say, "Go ahead and do what you doing. You is your
father child, you hear, not mine."

The real split between my mother and me happened not in
Miguel Street, but in the country.

My mother had decided to leave my father, and she wanted
to take me to her mother.

I refused to go.

My father was ill, and in bed. Besides, he had promised that
if I stayed with him I was to have a whole box of crayons.

I chose the crayons and my father.

We were living at the time in Cunupia, where my father was
a driver on the sugar estates. He wasn't a slave-driver, but a driver
of free people, but my father used to behave as though the people
were slaves. He rode about the estates on a big clumsy brown
horse, cracking his whip at the labourers and people said – I really
don't believe this – that he used to kick the labourers.

I don't believe it because my father had lived all his life in
Cunupia and he knew that you really couldn't push the Cunupia
people around. They are not tough people, but they think nothing
of killing, and they are prepared to wait years for the chance to
kill someone they don't like. In fact, Cunupia and Tableland are
the two parts of Trinidad where murders occur often enough to
ensure quick promotion for the policemen stationed there.

At first we lived in the barracks, but then my father wanted to
move to a little wooden house not far away.

My mother said, "You playing hero. Go and live in your house
by yourself, you hear."

She was afraid, of course, but my father insisted. So we moved to the house, and then trouble really started.

A man came to the house one day about midday and said to my mother, "Where your husband?"

My mother said. "I don't know."

The man was cleaning his teeth with a twig from a hibiscus plant. He spat and said, "It don't matter. I have time. I could wait."

My mother said, "You ain't doing nothing like that. I know what you thinking, but I have my sister coming here right now."

The man laughed and said, "I not doing anything. I just want to know when he coming home."

I began to cry in terror.

The man laughed.

My mother said, "Shut up this minute or I gave you something really to cry about."

I went to another room and walked about saying, "Rama! Rama! Sita Rama!" This was what my father had told me to say when I was in danger of any sort.

I looked out of the window. It was bright daylight, and hot, and there was nobody else in all the wide world of bush and trees.

And then I saw my aunt walking up the road.

She came and she said, "Anything wrong with you here? I was at home just sitting quite quiet, and I suddenly feel that something was going wrong. I feel I had to come to see."

The man said, "Yes, I know the feeling."

My mother, who was being very brave all the time, began to cry.

But all this was only to frighten us, and we were certainly frightened. My father always afterwards took his gun with him, and my mother kept a sharpened cutlass by her hand.

Then, at night, there used to be voices, sometimes from the road, sometimes from the bushes behind the house. The voices came from people who had lost their way and wanted lights, people who had come to tell my father that his sister had died suddenly in Debe, people who had come just to tell my father that there was a big fire at the sugar-mill. Sometimes there would be two or three of these voices, speaking from different directions, and we would sit awake in the dark house, just waiting, waiting for the voices to fall silent. And when they did fall silent it was even more terrible.

My father used to say, "They still outside. They want you to go out and look."

And at four or five o'clock when the morning lights was coming up we would hear the tramp of feet in the bush, feet going away.

As soon as darkness fell we would lock ourselves up in the house, and wait. For days there would sometimes be nothing at all, and then we would hear them again.

My father brought home a dog one day. We called it Tarzan. He was more of a playful dog than a watch-dog, a big hairy brown dog, and I would ride on its back.

When evening came I said, "Tarzan coming in with us?"

He wasn't. He remained whining outside the door, scratching it with his paws.

Tarzan didn't last long.

One morning we found him hacked to pieces and flung on the top step.

We hadn't heard any noise the night before.

My mother began to quarrel with my father, but my father was behaving as though he didn't really care what happened to him or to any of us.

My mother used to say, "You playing brave. But bravery ain't going to give any of us life, you hear. Let us leave this place."

My father began hanging up words of hope on the walls of the house, things from the Gita and the Bible, and sometimes things he had just made up.

He also lost his temper more often with my mother, and the time came when as soon as she entered a room he would scream and pelt things at her.

So she went back to her mother and I remained with my father.

During those days my father spent a lot of his time in bed, and so I had to lie down with him. For the first time I really talked to my father. He taught me three things.

The first was this.

"Boy," my father asked, "Who is your father?"

I said, "You is my father."

"Wrong."

"How that wrong?"

My father said, "You want to know who your father really is? God is your father."

"And what you is, then?"

"Me, what I is? I is – let me see, well, I is just a second sort of father, not your real father."

This teaching was later to get me into trouble, particularly with my mother.

The second thing my father taught me was the law of gravity.

We were sitting on the edge of the bed, and he dropped the box of matches.

He asked, "Now, boy, tell me why the matches drop."

I said, "But they bound to drop. What you want them to do? Go sideways?"

My father said, "I will tell why they drop. They drop because of the laws of gravity."

And he showed me a trick. He half filled a bucket with water and spun the bucket fast over his shoulder.

He said, "Look, the water wouldn't fall."

But it did. He got a soaking and the floor was wet.

He said, "It don't matter. I just put too much water, that's all. Look again,"

The second time it worked.

The third thing my father taught me was the blending of colours. This was just a few days before he died. He was very ill, and he used to spend a lot of time shivering and mumbling; and even when he fell asleep I used to hear him groaning.

I remained with him on the bed most of the time.

He said to me one day, "You got the coloured pencils?"

I took them from under the pillow.

He said. "You want to see some magic?"

I said, "What, you know magic really?"

He took the yellow pencil and filled in a yellow square.

He asked, "Boy, what colour this is?"

I said, "Yellow."

He said, "Just pass me the blue pencil now, and shut your eyes tight tight."

When I opened my eyes he said, "Boy, what colour this square is now?"

I said, "You sure you ain't cheating?"

He laughed and showed me how blue and yellow make green.

I said. "You mean if I take a leaf and wash it and wash it and wash it really good, it go be yellow or blue when I finish with it?"

He said, "No. You see, is God who blend those colours. God, your father."

I spent a lot of my time trying to make up tricks. The only one I could do was to put two match-heads together, light them, and make them stick. But my father knew that. But at last I found a trick that I was sure my father didn't know. He never got to know about it because he died on the night I was to show it him.

It had been a day of great heat, and in the afternoon the sky had grown low and heavy and black. It felt almost chilly in the house, and my father was sitting wrapped up in the rocking chair. The rain began to fall drop by heavy drop, beating like a hundred fists on the roof. It grew dark and I lit the oil lamp, sticking a pin in the wick, to keep away bad spirits from the house.

My father suddenly stopped rocking and whispered, "Boy, they here tonight. Listen. Listen."

We were both silent and I listened carefully, but my ears could catch nothing but the wind and the rain.

A window banged itself open. The wind whooshed in with heavy raindrops.

"God!" my father screamed.

I went to the window. It was a pitch black night, and the world was a wild and lonely place, with only the wind and the rain on the leaves. I had to fight to pull the window in, and before I could close it, I saw the sky light up with a crack of lightning.

I shut the window and waited for the thunder.

It sounded like a steamroller on the roof.

My father said, "Boy, don't frighten. Say what I tell you to say."

I went and sat at the foot of the rocking chair and I began to say, "Rama! Rama! Sita Rama!"

My father joined in. He was shivering with cold and fright.

Suddenly he shouted, "Boy, they here. They here. I hear them talking under the house. They could do what they like in all this noise and nobody could hear them."

I said, "Don't fraid, I have this cutlass here, and you have your gun."

But my father wasn't listening.

He said, "But it dark, man. It so dark. It so dark."

I got up and went to the table for the oil lamp to bring it nearer. But just then there was an explosion of thunder so low it might have been just above the roof. It rolled and rumbled for a long time. Then another window blew open and the oil lamp was blown out. The wind and the rain tore into the dark room.

My father screamed out once more, "Oh God, it dark."

I was lost in the black world. I screamed until the thunder died away and the rain had become a drizzle. I forgot all about the trick I had prepared for my father: the soap I had rubbed into the palms of my hands until it had dried and disappeared.

Everybody agreed on one thing. My mother and I had to leave the country. Port of Spain was the safest place. There was too a lot of laughter against my father, and it appeared that for the rest of my life I would have to bear the cross of a father who died from fright. But in a month or so I had forgotten my father, and I had begun to look upon myself as the boy who had no father. It seemed natural.

In fact, when we moved to Port of Spain and I saw what the normal relationship between father and son was – it was nothing more than the relationship between the beater and the beaten – when I saw this I was grateful.

My mother made a great thing at first about keeping me in my place and knocking out all the nonsense my father had taught me, I don't know why she didn't try harder, but the fact is that she soon lost interest in me, and she let me run about the street, only rushing down to beat me from time to time.

Occasionally, though, she would take the old firm line.

One day she kept me home. She said, "No school for you today. I just sick of tying your shoe-laces for you. Today you go have to learn that!"

I didn't think she was being fair. After all, in the country none of us wore shoes and I wasn't used to them.

That day she beat me and beat me and made me tie knot after knot and in the end I still couldn't tie my shoe-laces. For years afterwards it was a great shame to me that I couldn't do a simple thing like that, just as how I couldn't peel an orange. But about the shoes I made up a little trick. I never made my mother buy shoes the correct size. I pretended that those shoes hurt, and I made her get me shoes a size or two bigger. Once the attendant had tied the laces up for me, I never undid them, and merely slipped my feet in and out of the shoes. To keep them on my feet, I stuck paper in the toes.

To hear my mother talk, you would think I was a freak. Nearly every little boy she knew was better and more intelligent. There was one boy she knew who helped his mother paint her house. There was another boy who could mend his own shoes. There was still another boy who at the age of thirteen was earning a good twenty dollars a month, while I was just idling and living off her blood.

Still, there were surprising glimpses of kindness.

There was the time, for instance, when I was cleaning some tumblers for her one Saturday morning. I dropped a tumbler and it broke. Before I could do anything about it my mother saw what had happened.

She said, "How you break it?"

I said, "It just slip off. It smooth smooth."

She said, "Is a lot of nonsense drinking from glass. They break up so easy."

And that was all. I got worried about my mother's health.

She was never worried about mine.

She thought that there was no illness in the world a stiff dose of hot Epsom Salts couldn't cure. That was a penance I had to endure once a month. It completely ruined my weekend. And if there was something she couldn't understand, she sent me to the Health Officer in Tragarete Road. That was an awful place. You waited and waited and waited before you went in to see the doctor.

Before you had time to say, "Doctor, I have a pain –" he would be writing out a prescription for you. And again you had to wait for the medicine. All the Health Office medicines were the same. Water and pink sediment half an inch thick.

Hat used to say of the Health Office, "The Government taking up faith healing."

My mother considered the Health Office a good place for me to go to. I would go there at eight in the morning and return any time after two in the afternoon. It kept me out of mischief, and it cost only twenty-four cents a year.

But you mustn't get the impression that I was a saint all the time. I wasn't. I used to have odd fits where I just couldn't take an order from anybody, particularly my mother. I used to feel that I would dishonour myself for life if I took anybody's orders. And life is a funny thing, really. I sometimes got these fits just when my mother was anxious to be nice to me.

The day after Hat rescued me from drowning at Docksite I wrote an essay for my schoolmaster on the subject, "A Day at the Seaside". I don't think any schoolmaster ever got an essay like that. I talked about how I was nearly drowned and how calmly I was facing death, with my mind absolutely calm, thinking, "Well, boy, this is the end." The teacher was so pleased he gave me ten marks out of twelve.

He said, "I think you are a genius."

When I went home I told my mother, "That essay I write today, I get ten out of twelve for it."

My mother said, "How you so bold-face to lie brave brave so in front of my face? You want me give you a slap to turn your face?"

In the end I convinced her.

She melted at once. She sat down in the hammock and said, "Come and sit down by me, son."

Just then the crazy fit came on me.

I got very angry for no reason at all and I said, "No, I not going to sit by you."

She laughed and coaxed.

And the angrier she made me.

Slowly the friendliness died away. It had become a struggle between two wills. I was prepared to drown rather than dishonour myself by obeying.

"I ask you to come and sit down here."

"I not sitting down."

"Take off your belt."

I took it off and gave it to her. She belted me soundly, and my nose bled, but still I didn't sit in the hammock.

At times like these I used to cry, without meaning it, "If my father was alive you wouldn't be behaving like this."

So she remained the enemy. She was someone from whom I was going to escape as soon as I grew big enough. That was, in fact, the main lure of adulthood.

Progress was sweeping through Port of Spain in those days. The Americans were pouring money into Trinidad and there was a lot of talk from the British about colonial development and welfare.

One of the visible signs of this progress was the disappearance of the latrines. I hated the latrines, and I used to wonder about the sort of men who came with their lorries at night and carted away the filth; and there was always the horrible fear of falling into a pit.

One of the first men to have decent lavatories built was Hat, and we made a great thing of knocking down his old latrine. All the boys and men went to give a hand. I was too small to give a hand, but I went to watch. The walls were knocked down one by one and in the end there was only one remaining.

Hat said, "Boys, let we try to knock this one down in one big piece."

And they did.

The wall swayed and began to fall.

I must have gone mad in that split second, for I did a Superman act and tried to prevent the wall falling.

I just remember people shouting, "O God! Look out!"

I was travelling in a bus, one of the green buses of Sam's Super Service, from Port of Spain to Petit Valley. The bus was full of old women in bright bandanas carrying big baskets of eddoes, yams, bananas, with here and there some chickens. Suddenly the old women all began chattering, and the chickens began squawking. My head felt as though it would split, but when I tried to shout at the old women I found I couldn't open my mouth. I tried again, but all I heard, more distinctly now, was the constant chattering.

Water was pouring down my face.

I was flat out under a tap and there were faces above me looking down.

Somebody shouted, "He recover. Is all right."

Hat said, "How you feeling?"

I said, trying to laugh, "I feeling all right."

Mrs Bhakcu said, "You have any pains?"

I shook my head.

But, suddenly, my whole body began to ache. I tried to move my hand and it hurt.

I said, "I think I break my hand."

But I could stand, and they made me walk into the house.

My mother came and I could see her eyes glassy and wet with tears.

Somebody, I cannot remember who, said, "Boy, you had your mother really worried."

I looked at her tears, and I felt I was going to cry too. I had discovered that she could be worried and anxious for me.

I wished I were a Hindu god at that moment, with two hundred arms, so that all two hundred could be broken, just to enjoy that moment, and to see again my mother's tears.

The Baker's Story

V.S. Naipaul *(Trinidad)*

Look at me. Black as the Ace of Spades, and ugly to match. Nobody looking at me would believe they looking at one of the richest men in this city of Port of Spain. Sometimes I find it hard to believe it myself, you know, especially when I go out on some of the holidays that I start taking the wife and children to these days, and I catch sight of the obzocky black face in one of those fancy mirrors that expensive hotels have all over the place, as if to spite people like me.

Now everybody – particularly black people – forever asking me how this thing start, and I does always tell them I make my dough from dough. Ha! You like that one? But how it start? Well, you hearing me talk, and I don't have to tell you I didn't have no education. In Grenada, where I come from – and that is one thing these Trinidad black people don't forgive a man for being: a black Grenadian – in Grenada I was one of ten children, I believe – everything kind of mix up out there – and I don't even know who was the feller who hit my mother. I believe he hit a lot of women in all the other parishes of that island, too, because whenever I go back to Grenada for one of those holidays I tell you about, people always telling me that I remind them of this one and that one, and they always mistaking me for a shop assistant whenever I in a shop. (If this thing go on, one day I going to sell somebody something, just for spite.) And even in Trinidad, whenever I run into another Grenadian, the same thing does happen.

Well, I don't know what happen in Grenada, but mammy bring me alone over to Trinidad when she was still young. I don't know what she do with the others, but perhaps they wasn't even she own. Anyway, she get a work with some white people in St Ann's. They give she a uniform; they give she three meals a day; and they give she a few dollars a month besides. Somehow she get another man, a real Trinidad 'rangoutang, and somehow, I don't know how, she get somebody else to look after me while she was living with this man, for the money and the food she was getting was scarcely enough to support this low-minded

55

Trinidad rango she take up with.

It used to have a Chinee shop not far from this new aunty I was living with, and one day, when the old girl couldn't find the cash no how to buy a bread – is a hell of a thing, come to think of it now, that it have people in this island who can't lay their hands on enough of the ready to buy a bread – well, when she couldn't buy this bread she send me over to this Chinee shop to ask for trust. The Chinee woman – eh, but how these Chinee people does make children! – was big like anything, and I believe I catch she at a good moment, because she say nothing doing, no trust, but if I want a little work that was different, because she want somebody to take some bread she bake for some Indian people. But how she could trust me with the bread? This was a question. And then I pull out my crucifix from under my dirty merino that was more holes than cloth and I tell she to keep it until I come back with the money for the bake bread. I don't know what sort of religion these Chinee people have, but that woman look impressed like anything. But she was smart, though. She keep the crucifix and she send me off with the bread, which was wrap up in a big old *châle-au-pain*,[1] just two or three floursack sew together. I collect the money, bring it back, and she give me back the crucifix with a few cents and a bread.

And that was how this thing really begin. I always tell black people that was God give me my start in life, and don't mind these Trinidadians who does always tell you that Grenadians always praying. Is a true thing, though, because whenever I in any little business difficulty even these days I get down bam! straight on my two knees and I start praying like hell, boy.

Well, so this thing went on, until it was a regular afternoon work for me to deliver people bread. The bakery uses to bake ordinary bread – hops and pan and machine – which they uses to sell to the poorer classes. And how those Chinee people uses to work! This woman, with she big-big belly, clothes all dirty, sweating in front of the oven, making all this bread and making all this money, and I don't know what they doing with it, because all the time they living poor-poor in the back room, with only a bed, some hammocks for the young ones, and a few boxes. I couldn't talk to the husband at all. He didn't know a word of English and all the writing he uses to write uses to be in Chinee. He was a thin nashy feller, with those funny flapping khaki short

[1] *châle-au-pain*: bread-sack.

pants and white merino that Chinee people always wear. He uses to work like a bitch, too. We Grenadians understand hard work, so that is why I suppose I uses to get on so well with these Chinee people, and that is why these lazy black Trinidadians so jealous of we. But was a funny thing. They uses to live so dirty. But the children, man, uses to leave that ramshackle old back room as clean as new bread, and they always had this neatness, always with their little pencil-case and their little rubbers and rulers and blotters, and they never losing anything. They leaving in the morning in one nice little line and in the afternoon they coming back in this same little line, still cool and clean, as though nothing at all touch them all day. Is something they could teach black people children.

But as I was saying this bakery uses to bake ordinary bread for the poorer classes. For the richer classes they uses to bake, too. But what they would do would be to collect the dough from those people house, bake it, and send it back as bread, hot and sweet. I uses to fetch and deliver for this class of customer. They never let me serve in the shop; it was as though they couldn't trust me selling across the counter and collecting money in that rush. Always it had this rush. You know black people: even if it only have one man in the shop he always getting on as if it have one hell of a crowd.

Well, one day when I deliver some bread in this *châle-au-pain* to a family, there was a woman, a neighbour, who start saying how nice it is to get bread which you knead with your own hands and not mix up with all sort of people sweat. And this give me the idea. A oven is a oven. It have to go on, whether it baking one bread or two. So I tell this woman, was a Potogee woman, that I would take she dough and bring it back bake for she, and that it would cost she next to nothing. I say this in a sort of way that she wouldn't know whether I was going to give the money to the Chinee people, or whether it was going to cost she next to nothing because it would be I who was going to take the money. But she give me a look which tell me right away that she wanted me to take the money. So matter fix. So. Back in the *châle-au-pain* the next few days I take some dough, hanging it in the carrier of the bakery bicycle. I take it inside, as though I just didn't bother to wrap up the *châle-au-pain*, and the next thing is that this dough mix up with the other dough, and see me kneading and baking, as though all is one. The thing is, when you go in for a thing like that, to go in brave-brave. It have some people who make so much fuss when they doing one little thing that they bound to get catch. So, and I was surprise like hell, mind you. I get this stuff push in the oven, and is this said Chinee man, always with this sad and sorrowful Chinee face, who pulling it out of the oven with the long-handle shovel, looking at it, and pushing it back in.

And when I take the bread back, with some other bread, I collect the money cool-cool. The thing with a thing like this is that once you start is damn hard to stop. You start calculating this way and that way. And I have a calculating mind. I forever sitting down and working out how much say .50 a day every day for seven days, and every week for a year, coming to. And so this thing get to be a big thing with me. I wouldn't recommend this to any and everybody who want to go into business. But is what I mean when I tell people that I make my dough by dough.

The Chinee woman wasn't too well now. And the old man was getting on a little funny in a Chinee way. You know how those Chinee fellers does gamble. You drive past Marine Square in the early hours of the Sabbath and is two to one if you don't see some of those Chinee fellers sitting down outside the Treasury, as though they want to be near money, and gambling like hell. Well, the old man was gambling and the old girl was sick, and I was pretty well the only person looking after the bakery. I work damn hard for them, I could tell you. I even pick up two or three words of Chinee, and some of those rude black people start calling me Black Chinee, because at this time I was beginning to dress in short khaki pants and merino like a Chinee and I was drinking that tea Chinee people drinking all day long and I was walking and not saying much like a Chinee. And, now, don't believe what these black people say about Chinee and prejudice, eh. They have nothing at all against black people, provided they is hard-working and grateful.

But life is a funny thing. Now when it look that I all set, that everything going fine and dandy, a whole set of things happen that start me bawling. First, the Chinee lady catch a pleurisy and dead. Was a hell of a thing, but what else you expect when she was always bending down in front of that fire and then getting wet and going out in the dew and everything, and then always making these children too besides. I was sorry like hell, and a little frighten. Because I wasn't too sure how I was going to manage alone with the old man. All the time I work with him he never speak one word straight to me, but he always talking to me through his wife.

And now, look at my crosses. As soon as the woman dead, the Chinee man like he get mad. He didn't cry or anything like that, but he start gambling like a bitch, and the upshot was that one day, perhaps about a month after the old lady dead, the man tell his children to pack up and start leaving, because he gamble and lose the shop to another Chinee feller. I didn't know where I was standing, and nobody telling me nothing. They only packing. I don't know, I suppose they begin to feel that I was just part of the shop, and the old man not even saying that he sorry he lose me. And, you know, as soon as I drop to my knees and start praying, I see it was really God who right from the start put that idea of the dough in my head, because without that I would have been nowhere at all. Because the new feller who take over the shop say he don't want me. He was going to close the bakery and set up a regular grocery, and he didn't want me serving there because the grocery customers wouldn't like black people serving them. So look at me. Twenty-three years old and no work. No nothing. Only I have this Chinee-ness and I know how to bake bread and I have this extra bit of cash I save up over the years.

I slip out of the old khaki short pants and merino and I cruise around the town a little, looking for work. But nobody want bakers. I had about $700.00, and I see that this cruising around would do but it wouldn't pay, because the money was going fast. Now look at this. You know, it never cross my mind in those days that I could open a shop of my own. Is how it is with black people. They get so use to working for other people that they get to believe that because they black they can't do nothing else but work for other people. And I must tell you that when I start praying and God tell me to go out and open a shop for myself I feel that perhaps God did mistake or that I hadn't hear Him good. Because God only saying to me, "Youngman, take your money and open a bakery. You could bake good bread." He didn't say to open a parlour, which a few black fellers do, selling rock cakes and mauby and other soft drinks. No, He say open a bakery. Look at my crosses.

I had a lot of trouble borrowing the extra few hundred dollars, but I eventually get a Indian feller to lend me. And this is what I always tell young fellers. That getting credit ain't no trouble at all if you know exactly what you want to do. I didn't go round telling people to lend me money because I want to build house or buy lorry. I just did want to bake bread. Well, to cut a long story short, I buy a break-down old place near Arouca, and I spend most of what I had trying to fix the place up. Nothing extravagant, you understand, because Arouca is Arouca and you don't want to frighten off the country-bookies with anything too sharp. Too besides, I didn't have the cash. I just put in a few second-hand glass cases and things like that. I write up my name on a board, and look, I in business.

Now the funny thing happen. In Laventille the people couldn't have enough of the bread I was baking – and in the last few months was me was doing the baking. But now trouble. I baking better bread than the people of Arouca ever see, and I can't get one single feller to come in like man through my rickety old front door and buy a penny hops bread. You hear all this talk about quality being its own advertisement? Don't believe it, boy. Is quality plus something else. And I didn't have this something else. I begin to wonder what the hell it could be. I say is because I new in Arouca that this thing happening. But no, I new, I get stale, and the people not flocking in their hundreds to the old shop. Day after day I baking two or three quarts good and all this just remaining and going dry and stale, and the only bread I selling is to the man from the government farm, buying stale cakes and bread for the cows or pigs or whatever they have up there. And was good bread. So I get down on the old knees and I pray as though I want to wear them out. And still I getting the same answer: "Youngman" – was always the way I uses to get call in these prayers – "Youngman, you just bake bread."

Pappa! This was a thing. Interest on the loan piling up every month. Some months I borrow from aunty and anybody else who kind enough to listen just to pay off the interest. And things get so low that I uses to have to go out and pretend to people that I was working for another man bakery and that I was going to bake their dough cheap-cheap. And in Arouca cheap mean cheap. And the little cash I picking up in this disgraceful way was just about enough to keep the wolf from the door, I tell you.

Jeezan. Look at confusion. The old place in Arouca so damn out of the way – was why I did buy it, too, thinking that they didn't have no bakery there and that they would be glad of the good Grenadian-baked – the place so out of the way nobody would want to buy it. It ain't even insure or anything, so it can't get in a little fire accident or anything – not that I went in for that sort of thing. And every time I go down on my knees, the answer coming straight back at me: "Youngman, you just bake bread."

Well, for the sake of the Lord I baking one or two quarts regular every day, though I begin to feel that the Lord want to break me, and I begin to feel too that this was His punishment for what I uses to do to the Chinee people in their bakery. I was beginning to feel bad and real ignorant. I uses to stay away from the bakery after baking those quarts for the Lord – nothing to lock up, nothing to thief – and, when any of the Laventille boys drop in on the way to Manzanilla and Balandra and those other beaches on the Sabbath, I uses to tell them, making a joke out of it, that I was "loafing". They uses to laugh like hell, too. It have nothing in the whole world so funny as to see a man you know flat out on his arse and catching good hell.

The Indian feller was getting anxious about his cash, and you couldn't blame him, either, because some months now he not even seeing his interest. And this begin to get me down, too. I remember how all the man did ask me when I went to him for money was: "You sure you want to bake bread? You feel you have a hand for baking bread?" And yes-yes, I tell him, and just like that he shell out the cash. And now he was getting anxious. So one day, after baking those loaves for the Lord, I take a Arima Bus Service bus to Port of Spain to see this feller. I was feeling brave enough on the way. But as soon as I see the old sea and get a whiff of South Quay and the bus touch the Railway Station terminus my belly start going pweh-pweh. I decide to roam about the city for a little.

Was a hot morning, *petit-carême*[1] weather, and in those days a coconut uses still to cost .04. Well, it had this coconut cart in the old square and I stop by it. It was a damn funny thing to see. The seller was a black feller. And you wouldn't know how funny this was, unless you know that every coconut seller in the island is Indian. They have this way of handling a cutlass that black people don't have. Coconut in left hand; with right hand bam, bam, bam with cutlass, and coconut cut open, ready to drink. I ain't never see a coconut seller chop his hand. And here was this black feller doing this bam-bam business on a coconut with a cutlass. It was as funny as seeing a black man wearing dhoti and turban. The sweetest part of the whole business was that this black feller was, forgetting looks, just like an Indian. He was

[1] *petit-carême*: the kind of weather just before Easter time.

talking Hindustani to a lot of Indian fellers, who was giving him jokes like hell, but he wasn't minding. It does happen like that sometimes with black fellers who live a lot with Indians in the country. They putting away curry, talking Indian, and behaving just like Indians. Well, I take a coconut from this black man and then went on to see the feller about the money.

He was more sad than vex when I tell him, and if I was in his shoes I woulda be sad, too. Is a hell of a thing when you see your money gone and you ain't getting the sweet little kisses from the interest every month. Anyway, he say he would give me three more months' grace, but that if I didn't start shelling out at the agreed rate he would have to foreclose. "You put me in a hell of a position." he say. "Look at me. You think I want a shop in Arouca?"

I was feeling a little better when I leave the feller, and who I should see when I leave but Percy. Percy was an old rango who uses to go to the Laventille elementary school with me. I never know a boy get so much cut-arse as Percy. But he grow up real hard and ignorant with it, and now he wearing fancy clothes like a saga boy, and talking about various business offers. I believe he was selling insurance – is a thing that nearly every idler doing in Trinidad, and, mark my words, the day coming when you going to see those fellers trying to sell insurance to one another. Anyway, Percy getting on real flash, and he say he want to stand me a lunch for old times' sake. He makes a few of the usual ignorant Trinidadian jokes about Grenadians, and we went up to the Angostura Bar. I did never go there before, and wasn't the sort of place you would expect a rango like Percy to be welcome. But we went up there and Percy start throwing his weight around with the waiters, and, mind you, they wasn't even a quarter as black as Percy. Is a wonder they didn't abuse him. especially with all those fair people around. After the drinks Percy say, "Where you want to have this lunch?"

Me, I don't know a thing about the city restaurants, and when Percy talk about food all I was expecting was rice and peas or a roti off a Indian stall or a mauby and rock cake in some parlour. And is a damn hard thing to have people, even people as ignorant as Percy, showing off on you, especially when you carrying two nails in your pocket to make the jingling noise. So I tell Percy we could go to a parlour or a bar. But he say, "No, no. When I treat my friends, I don't like black people meddling with my food."

And was only then that the thing hit me. I suppose that what

Trinidadians say about the stupidness of Grenadians have a little truth, though you have to live in a place for a long time before you get to know it really well. Then the thing hit me, man.

When black people in Trinidad go to a restaurant they don't like to see black people meddling with their food. And then I see that though Trinidad have every race and every colour, every race have to do special things. But look, man. If you want to buy a snowball, who you buying it from? You wouldn't buy it from a Indian or a Chinee or a Potogee. You would buy it from a black man. And I myself, when I was getting my place in Arouca fix up, I didn't employ Indian carpenters or masons. If a Indian in Trinidad decide to go into the carpentering business the man would starve. Who ever see a Indian carpenter? I suppose the only place in the world where they have Indian carpenters and Indian masons is India. Is a damn funny thing. One of these days I must make a trip to that country, to just see this thing. And as we walking I see the names of bakers: Coelho, Pantin, Stauble. Potogee or Swiss, or something, and then all those other Chinee places. And, look at the laundries. If a black man open a laundry, you would take your clothes to it? *I* wouldn't take my clothes there. Well, I walking to this restaurant, but I jumping for joy. And then all sorts of things fit into place. You remember that the Chinee people didn't let me serve bread across the counter? I uses to think it was because they didn't trust me with the rush. But it wasn't that. It was that, if they did let me serve, they would have had no rush at all. You ever see anybody buying their bread off a black man?

I ask Percy why he didn't like black people meddling with his food in public places. The question throw him a little. He stop and think and say. "It don't *look* nice."

Well, you could guess the rest of the story. Before I went back to Arouca that day I made contact with a yellow boy call Macnab. This boy was half black and half Chinee, and, though he had a little brown colour and the hair a little curly, he could pass for one of those Cantonese. They a little darker than the other Chinee people, I believe. Macnab I find beating a steel pan in somebody yard – they was practising for Carnival – and I suppose the only reason that Macnab was willing to come all the way to Arouca was because he was short of the cash to buy his costume for the Carnival island.

But he went up with me. I put him in front of the shop, give

give him a merino and a pair of khaki short pants, and tell him to talk as Chinee as he could, if he wanted to get that Carnival bonus. I stay in the back room, and I start baking bread. I even give Macnab a old Chinee paper, not to read, because Macnab could scarcely read English, but just to leave lying around, to make it look good. And I get hold of one of those big Chinese calendars with Chinee women and flowers and waterfalls and hang it up on the wall. And when this was all ready, I went down on my knees and thank God. And still the old message coming, but friendly and happy now: "Youngman, you just bake bread."

And, you know, that solve another problem. I was worrying to hell about the name I should give the place. New Shanghai, Canton, Hongkong, Nanking, Yang-tse-Kiang. But when the old message came over I know right away what the name should be. I scrub off the old name – no need to tell you what that was – and I get a proper sign painter to copy a few letters from the Chinee newspaper. Below that, in big letters, I make him write:

YUNG MAN BAKER

I never show my face in the front of the shop again. And I tell you, without boasting, that I bake damn good bread. And the people of Arouca ain't that foolish. They know a good thing. And soon I was making so much money that I was able to open a branch in Arima and then another in Port of Spain self. Was hard in the beginning to get real Chinee people to work for a black man. But money have it own way of talking, and when today you pass any of the Yung Man establishments all you seeing behind the counter is Chinee. Some of them ain't even know they working for a black man. My wife handling that side of the business, and the wife is Chinee. She come from down Cedros way. So look at me now, in Port of Spain, giving Stauble and Pantin and Coelho a run for their money. As I say, I only going in the shops from the back. But every Monday morning I walking brave brave to Marine Square and going in the bank, from the front.

The Raffle

V.S. Naipaul *(Trinidad)*

They don't pay primary schoolteachers a lot in Trinidad, but they allow them to beat their pupils as much as they want.

Mr Hinds, my teacher, was a big beater. On the shelf below *The Last of England* he kept four or five tamarind[1] rods. They are good for beating. They are limber, they sting and they last. There was a tamarind tree in the schoolyard. In his locker Mr Hinds also kept a leather strap soaking in the bucket of water every class had in case of fire.

It wouldn't have been so bad if Mr Hinds hadn't been so young and athletic. At the one school sports I went to, I saw him slip off shining shoes, roll up his trousers neatly to mid-shin and win the Teachers' Hundred Yards, a cigarette between his lips, his tie flapping smartly over his shoulder. It was a wine-coloured tie: Mr Hinds was careful about his dress. That was something else that somehow added to the terror. He wore a brown suit, a cream shirt and the wine-coloured tie.

It was also rumoured that he drank heavily at weekends.

But Mr Hinds had a weak spot. He was poor. We knew he gave those "private lessons" because he needed the extra money. He gave us private lessons in the ten-minute morning recess. Every boy paid fifty cents for that. If a boy didn't pay, he was kept in all the same and flogged until he paid.

We also knew that Mr Hinds had an allotment in Morvant where he kept some poultry and a few animals.

The other boys sympathised with us – needlessly, Mr Hinds beat us, but I believe we were all a little proud of him.

I say he beat us, but I don't really mean that. For some reason which I could never understand then and can't now, Mr Hinds never beat me. He never made me clean the blackboard. He never made me shine his shoes with the duster. He even called me by my first name, Vidiadhar.

This didn't do me any good with the other boys. At cricket I wasn't allowed to bowl or keep wicket and I always went in at

[1] *tamarind*: tropical tree with fruit used for making drinks.

number eleven. My consolation was that I was spending only two terms at the school before going on to Queen's Royal College. I didn't want to go to QRC so much as I wanted to get away from Endeavour (that was the name of the school). Mr Hind's favour made me feel insecure.

At private lessons one morning Mr Hinds announced that he was going to raffle a goat – a shilling a chance.

He spoke with a straight face and nobody laughed. He made me write out the names of all the boys in the class on two foolscap sheets. Boys who wanted to risk a shilling had to put a tick after their names. Before private lessons ended there was a tick after every name.

I became very unpopular. Some boys didn't believe there was a goat. They all said that if there was a goat, they knew who was going to get it. I hoped they were right. I had long wanted an animal of my own, and the idea of getting milk from my own goat attracted me. I had heard that Mannie Ramjohn, Trinidad's champion miler, trained on goat's milk and nuts.

Next morning I wrote out the names of the boys on slips of paper. Mr Hinds borrowed my cap, put the slips in, took one out, said, "Vidiadhar, is your goat;" and immediately threw all the slips into the wastepaper basket.

At lunch I told my mother, "I win a goat today."

"What sort of goat?"

"I don't know. I ain't see it."

She laughed. She didn't believe in the goat, either. But when she finished she said: "It would be nice, though."

I was getting not to believe in the goat, too. I was afraid to ask Mr Hinds, but a day or two later he said, "Vidiadhar, you coming or you ain't coming to get your goat?"

He lived in a tumbledown wooden house in Woodbrook and when I got there I saw him in khaki shorts, vest and blue canvas shoes. He was cleaning his bicycle with a yellow flannel. I was overwhelmed. I had never associated him with such dress and such a menial labour. But his manner was more ironic and dismissing than in the classroom.

He led me to the back of the yard. There *was* a goat. A white one with big horns, tied to a plum tree. The ground around the tree was filthy. The goat looked sullen and sleepy-eyed, as if a little stunned by the smell it had made. Mr Hinds invited me to stroke the goat. I stroked it. He closed his eyes and went on chewing. When I stopped stroking him, he opened his eyes.

66

Every afternoon at about five an old man drove a donkey-cart through Miguel Street where we lived. The cart was piled with fresh grass tied into neat little bundles, so neat you felt grass wasn't a thing that grew but was made in a factory somewhere. That donkey-cart became important to my mother and me. We were buying five, sometimes six bundles a day, and every bundle cost six cents. The goat didn't change. He still looked sullen and bored. From time to time Mr Hinds asked me with a smile how the goat was getting on, and I said it was getting on fine. But when I asked my mother when we were going to get milk from the goat she told me to stop aggravating her. Then one day she put up a sign:

RAM FOR SERVICE
Apply Within For Terms

and got very angry when I asked her to explain it.

The sign made no difference. We bought the neat bundles of grass, the goat ate, and I saw no milk.

And when I got home one lunch-time I saw no goat.

"Somebody borrow it," my mother said. She looked happy.

"When it coming back?"

She shrugged her shoulders.

It came back that afternoon. When I turned the corner into Miguel Street I saw it on the pavement outside our house. A man I didn't know was holding it by a rope and making a big row, gesticulating like anything with his free hand. I knew that sort of man. He wasn't going to let hold of the rope until he had said his piece. A lot of people were looking on through curtains.

"But why all-you want to rob poor people so?" he said, shouting. He turned to his audience behind the curtains. "Look, all-you, just look at this goat!"

The goat, limitlessly impassive, chewed slowly, its eyes half-closed.

"But how all you people so advantageous? My brother stupid and he ain't know this goat but I know this goat. Everybody in Trinidad who know about goat know this goat, from Icacos to Mayaro to Toco to Chaguaramas," he said, naming the four corners of Trinidad. "Is the most uselessest goat in the whole world. And you charge my brother for this goat? Look, you better give me back my brother money, you hear."

My mother looked hurt and upset. She went inside and came

out with some dollar notes. The man took them and handed over the goat.

That evening my mother said, "Go and tell your Mr Hinds that I don't want this goat here."

Mr Hinds didn't look surprised. "Don't want it, eh?" He thought, and passed a well-trimmed thumb-nail over his moustache. "Look, tell you. Going to buy him back. Five dollars."

I said, "He eat more than that in grass alone."

That didn't surprise him either. "Say six, then."

I sold. That, I thought, was the end of that.

One Monday afternoon about a month before the end of my last term I announced to my mother, "That goat raffling again."

She becamed alarmed.

At tea on Friday I said casually, "I win the goat."

She was expecting it. Before the sun set a man had brought the goat away from Mr Hinds, given my mother some money and taken the goat away.

I hoped Mr Hinds would never ask about the goat. He did, though. Not the next week, but the week after that, just before school broke up.

I didn't know what to say.

But a boy called Knolly, a fast bowler and a favourite victim of Mr Hinds, answered for me. "What goat?" he whispered loudly. "That goat kill and eat long time."

Mr Hinds was suddenly furious. "Is true, Vidiadhar?"

I didn't nod or say anything. The bell rang and saved me.

At lunch I told my mother, "I don't want to go back to that school."

She said, "You must be brave."

I didn't like the argument, but went.

We had Geography the first period.

"Naipaul," Mr Hinds said right away, forgetting my first name, "define a peninsula."

"Peninsula," I said, "a piece of land entirely surrounded by water."

"Good. Come up here." He went to the locker and took out the soaked leather strap. Then he fell on me. "You sell my goat?" Cut. "You kill my goat?" Cut. "How you so damn ungrateful?" Cut, cut, cut. "Is the last time you win anything I raffle."

It was the last day I went to that school.

The Visitor

H. Orlando Patterson *(Jamaica)*

He was odd. Below his grey, felt hat he had an uncertain smile which confused me a little as I somehow got the strange impression that I was making him uncomfortable. He remained silent for a long time. I began to detect something sinister about him.

Suddenly, he said, in an almost apologetic voice, "You Miss Glady's son?" There was a faint smell of rum and toothpaste. I nooded. He kept staring at me; his mouth remained slightly open. His eyes were watery, curious and a little sad.

"You want me to call her for you?" I asked.

"What?" He seemed surprised that I was capable of asking a question; or perhaps that I had been daring enough to put one to him. He swallowed, stared at me with even greater curiosity, and then murmured. "Oh, call her? Yes, yes, do that."

What a funny man, I thought, as I went to the door.

"Mamma."

"What?"

"A man out here to see you."

"A man? Which man that?"

"Don't know him. Never seen him before."

She got up and peeped through the window. By now I was anxious myself to know who the stranger might be and so I observed her closely as she peered outside at him. She stared and stared. She did not move and seemed petrified by the window. I walked inside and had a mild shock as I saw her expression.

"What happen, Mamma?"

She did not answer. I realised that something was very wrong. I had never known her to be confronted with a situation which she seemed in any way incapable of handling. Not until that moment.

"Mamma . . . ?"

"Go an' tell 'im me not here . . . go an' tell 'im . . . no, wait, tell 'im . . . tell 'im me coming."

Whoever the stranger was I realised that he somehow threatened us and instinctively began to fear him. Yet, when I walked back to him his appearance instilled little apprehension in me.

69

His manner was uncertain, vague and distant. It reassured me against my every instinct. I even had, for a moment, the absurd impression that he was afraid of us. And this flattered my childhood pride.

"My mother says she coming." I told him.

He said thanks softly. My mother walked out of the door, then stopped and continued to stare at him. He walked towards her and stopped a few yards away. A conspiracy of silence seemed to reign between them, between us I should say, for by now I too was left simply staring, wondering what it was all about. It was he who finally broke the silence.

"Hi, Gladys. I hope I didn't surprise you too much?"

"How you find where I live?" Her voice was unusually restrained, though there was an ever so slight note of threat in it.

"Oh, I was jus' passing through the town. I ask at the China-man shop if they know you, an' they show me the way. ...."

After another long pause she beckoned to him to come inside. The door remained half-closed and I remained staring at it for the next fifteen minutes. Then I heard my mother calling me. My heart leapt at the thought of finally solving the mystery of the stranger. I found myself stuffing my shirt into my trousers respectfully. My mother called again, impatiently. I ran inside.

He was sitting on the only chair we had; she was on the edge of the bed. They both looked at me as I entered. I made sure to avoid his eyes, staring at her for refuge. Then after another long pause, she beckoned to him hesitantly and mumbled, "Your father."

I was a little surprised, of course, but not shocked. Perhaps more confused than anything else. I had known he existed somewhere in some shape. But my conception of him had been vague, formless. He had been part of my own personal folk-lore: something I had liked and at times dreamt about, like expensive gold-fish, but never really desired, never took quite seriously. Seeing him there before me, I was sure I would have been no less confounded had I been faced with Humpty-Dumpty. What could I say? What was I expected to say? They expected me to look at him. Well, I looked at him.

He had lines on his brow and his cheeks were rough. I thought he must shave every day; my friends had told me their fathers did. I thought it would have been very funny if my mother had had to shave every day too; I was not unconscious of my stupid notion.

He nodded in a gesture of approval as he stared at me.

"You are a fine boy," he said; and I wondered what he meant.

Then he looked at my mother and in the same uncertain, unconvincing voice, he repeated, "He's a fine boy."

My mother murmured something in response, then glanced at me. Her eyes lacked the proud gleam of satisfaction which it usually bore when someone flattered me in this manner. Instead, it was slightly censorious:[1] I could detect a hint of anger in them and I felt lost to explain why she should have reacted in this manner. When she looked away she held down her head, and if I hadn't known her so well I would have been convinced that there was shame in her eyes. After that she rested her elbow on her knee and her chin between her fingers and sighed, which I knew, was her silent, physical way of repeating an expression that was always on her lips: "Oh, what a life, my God!"

I kept wondering what was going on. I had observed adults to act in the strangest way before; but underlying my ignorance, there had always been some gleam of understanding, some awareness, if ever so remote, that whatever they were up to was somehow meaningful. But the behaviour of my mother and the stranger now completely baffled me. Why didn't they say something? Did they hate each other? Did the fact that he was my father mean all that much to her?

Suddenly, I was overwhelmed with the fear that he had come to take her away from me. Perhaps it was that which was worrying them. They did not know how to tell me. My mother would be leaving me all alone. In an instant, the essence of my relationship with her, the importance of her presence, impressed itself on me. I neither love her nor hated her. I feared her a little, perhaps, for often she would beat me cruelly. But the rage I expressed then in my tears was purely an immediate reaction to the pain I felt. Somehow I conceived that beating me had meant far more to her than it had to me. The world was tough; so she often told me. I was her child and completely at her mercy; it was only natural. Despite everything, a strong bond held us together. Nothing positive, really; more the fear that if we lost each other we would have lost everything. For me she was the person I called mother: she gave me food, clothes and the books I read at school. And she taught me to be good. It was never quite clear what she meant by being good. More often than not, it simply meant *being good* to her, or not being ungrateful, which amounted to much the same thing. I suppose she could be said to have been warm in her own way.

[1]*censorious*: fault finding.

But unconsciously, she taught me not to expect very much and so I asked for very little. All I desired was for her to be there, always there. Now there was the threat of her departure.

But that was not possible. I reassured myself that I was being silly to the point of deciding that it would have been better if I left the room. Perhaps they wished to say adult things. As soon as I began to nudge my way to the door I heard him saying, in a manner which suggested that he was repeating himself, "Yes, it's been a long time, Gladys." I decided then that I was certainly the reason for their apparent discomfort, and I began to move less imperceptibly to the door. Suddenly I heard my mother call my name. Her voice was sharp and severe; she did not have to say that I must stay; her tone was enough.

The stranger looked at me quizzically,[2] then back at her and suddenly sprang out of his chair. He made the usual motions which indicated an intention to depart; yet, he hesitated. Then he suddenly seemed to remember something. He took out a five-shilling note from his trouser pocket and handed it to me.

"Buy a present with it," he said.

I stared at the note, a little shocked, both at the large sum of money and at the fact that he, of all people, should have given it to me. I looked up at my mother to see what her response was. I was not surprised when she said, "Give it back." Then she turned to him and said, "I bring 'im up all this time without your help; I don't need it now."

I immediately held the money out to him for I realised that my mother was in no mood to be crossed. I began to dread the moment when I would be alone with her.

The man began to protest, but he broke off suddenly and took back the note from me. I began to feel sorry for him, for he seemed insulted and sad. He took up his little felt hat, put it on his head and left without saying another word. I never saw him again.

---

[2]*quizzically*: questioningly.

The Bitter Choice

Clifford Sealy *(Trinidad)*

The oppressive midday heat beat fiercely down upon the withered blades of grass in Woodford Square,[1] the airy sanctuary of the intelligentsia[2] of Port of Spain's[1] unemployed. Unequal groups of ragged, melancholic, and vociferous men and women scattered themselves over the parched tract discussing one subject or another.

In one group, the absorbing subject was foreign politics; in another, careful consideration was being given to counsel's submissions in a case of murder then being heard; and in a third the Government's intervention in the existing water-front workers' strike was being animatedly debated.

There were as many topics of conversation as there were groups; and these topics were as varied in nature and enormity as the men who discussed them were in character and appearance. In the centre of the Square rose a small, green metal statue, encircled by a wide stone pond which was invariably empty. And facing this pond were six wooden benches whose coat of deep brown paint had long since vanished, exposing the rough yellow pitch-pine.

On one of these benches sat three men. Leo was in the middle. Tall and sturdy, he wore a faded and dirty khaki suit, which, by the vast areas of his arms and legs it left uncovered, gave evidence of an earlier association with a shorter and slimmer owner.

On Leo's right sat Eric. Lean and emaciated, his bones seemed to protrude through his thin, black skin, and a crafty glint shone in his ashen eyes.

Sam completed the triumvirate.[3] Short and slim, he was the least prepossessing, and his opinions always drifted between those of his two comrades.

[1]*Woodford Square*: A popular square in Port of Spain, the capital of Trinidad; a haunt for "park orators", unemployed men and passers-by.

[2]*intelligentsia*: group of people who consider themselves clever.

[3]*triumvirate*: In the days of Imperial Rome a triumvirate was the office or magistracy of a triumvir (one of *three* officers mutually exercising the same public function).

"I hear the Government want people for stevedore[4] work, boys," Eric ventured in a hoarse and insinuating tone.

Leo blew a thick cloud of smoke through his heavy, frog-like lips. Then, with the tip of the little finger of his right hand he flicked the grey ash from the end of his cigarette, lightly crushed out the dim red glow on the iron arm-rest of the bench, brushed away the black cinders and placed the still warm "zoot" behind his right ear.

He did not speak; nor did Sam, who with lowered head watched his stumpy fingers play with a loose shirt-button.

"What happen, now?" growled Eric, injured by this unanticipated silence. "All you ain't want work or what? The Government giving we work, and all you sitting down like all you proud!"

Leo was angered by Eric's sarcasm; and facing his companion, he shouted with a vehemence born of deep moral conviction, "We black people ain't have no unity! Anybody who take that kind of work want shooting! When the white man have he business, all of them does get together. But when we black people do something, the other set does get against them! We ain't have no unity, that is what!" he concluded, turning around again and wiping his oval, unshaven face with the sleeve of his jacket.

"You right, *oui*, Leo! You right, boy!" Sam chimed in uncertainly. "We black people really ain't have no love for one another. That is the real, real truth!"

"Don't mind Leo and he stupidness, man, Sam!" came Eric's admonishing voice. "He minding them politicians and their talk!"

"But what the man say yesterday is true, though," Leo put in.

"What he say? I wish I mind them and their talk! That ain't going to get you any place!" Rising from the bench and dusting the seat of his trousers with the palm of his hand, Eric continued, his crooked features contorting themselves into a contemptuous grimace: "Black people too damn foolish." And with a condescending pat on Leo's shoulder, he said as he departed, somewhat with the air of a wizened father to an imprudent son, "What you say is true; but politics ain't for black people. Man have to live."

Leo watched the lanky, half-stooping figure walk down the pathway, and he felt strangely towards him. Eric was depraved; that he knew. Yet, his words always inspired for themselves a queer respect in Leo's mind.

[4]*stevedore*: worker in the docks.

There was much activity in the Square at this hour. Shop assistants hurried backwards and forwards, going to and from their lunch. And there were also the shoppers: women, stout and thin, tall and short, with parcels hanging from their arms and gossip clinging to their tongues.

The clock of neighbouring Trinity Cathedral chimed twelve. It reminded Leo that soon he would have to face Mabel, his wife, who came from Grenada. The thought of Mabel sent his mind rolling backwards to the events of the past few days.

Life was hard. Life, he reflected, had never been rosy; now, however, it was coarse and horrid. And Mabel's callousness worsened matters. And slender hope there was of her changing since she had joined the "In Jesus Mighty Name" sect, a band of misguided poor people, who each in his distress fancied he had received a "call" to block the street corners at nights with prayer meetings.

Returning from her "lecture" yesterday afternoon, he recalled, she was distressingly hostile.

"When you going to get work, Leo?" she had asked him. "Is over a whole year you ain't working. How long you think we could live so?"

"But Mabel," he had reproached her, "I trying my best. Some people ain't working for years, now."

"That is some people," she had heatedly exploded, "but me is me. I can't go on living like this, not knowing what I go eat tomorrow, or when the man going to put we out for the rent, or borrowing and not knowing when I am going to pay back. This ain't go do."

"Keep courage, *doudou*,"[5] he had exhorted her, adding in an effort to mitigate her depression, "you forget is tomorrow I have to see the man at the Soap Factory."

Sam's squeaky voice drew Leo out of his meditations. "What about the job you was to get this morning, Leo? You ain't tell me nothing about it."

"The foreman's cousin already get it, man!" Leo told him.

"God-father, boy," Sam murmured understandingly, shaking his odd, round head from left to right, "God-father in everything, *oui*."

Presently, the number of persons travelling through the Square lessened, and the clouds of dust kicked up by their hasty steps

[5] *doudou*: Doux doux or doo doo: a term of endearment: like "darling".

dispersed. Occasionally, a bunch of baked and cracked leaves would lazily float to the ground; while above, the soft kissing of the trees could be heard.

Some of the groups broke up; but almost immediately new ones formed themselves in the same spots. Others, overcome by the scorching glare of the sun, sought shelter in the small, concrete bandstand. But the Square, then, as at all times throughout the day, retained its minimum population of fifty idle souls.

"We going see, tomorrow, old man," said Leo, rising from his seat.

"All right," Sam said.

Soon, Leo arrived at his barrack-room[6] in Duncan Street. Mabel was lying on the small iron bed, her cheap, green spotted dress combining picturesquely with the variegated colours of the fibre mattress. In her fat hands, wrinkled by continual laundering, reposed an expensively bound, black Bible.

Disappointment must clearly have been reflected in Leo's anguished features, for at sight of him, Mabel exclaimed, "You ain't get the job!"

"No!" Leo said.

"But this is ..." Mabel burst out, closing her Bible and rising to a sitting position. "What you mean by? If you know you can't get work, what you take wife for?"

His pride severely wounded, Leo spluttered, "But, Mabel, I trying me best."

"You trying you' best," she sneered. "How Jane's husband working on the wharf three days now?"

"He is a dog, you see!" growled Leo, getting up from the small wooden bench on which he sat, and which together with a dully varnished bureau and a rectangular dining-table comprised the entire household furniture. "I ain't want no work like that. He ..."

"Oh-oh, you' picking and choosing," she snarled, burying the knuckles of her fingers deeply into her sides. "You minding them Unions and their politics. I see. Is pride that have you going on so."

"It ain't pride. Is education. Education like the people in ..."

"Education what! Education could mind you?"

"You ain't understand ..."

---

[6]*barrack-room*: A tenement room.

"I understand, well. You ain't really want work. But I ain't living with no man who ain't want to work and mind his wife. I ain't any woman you just find, and you have to mind me." And with an air of dramatic finality, she added "If you ain't want to mind me, I go do it myself."

"What happen?"

"I'm very calm," Mabel replied, her beady black eyes glistening with defiance. "but if you ain't mind me, other people going to do it."

"Go to hell, he shouted, tumbling out of the room.

A huge and excited crowd had gathered in Prince Street. Men and women stood in the streets and on the pavements noisily speaking to each other. Some of them wore bands of various colours on their sleeveless arms; some held in their hands small galvanised buckets filled with water or canebaskets filled with food; others waved small cardboard placards splashed with bold red.

To Leo there was an infectious exultancy that seemed more appropriate to a Carnival sailors' band. He marvelled at the ease with which they fell into the military march and the unrestrained zeal with which they swung their banners.

As though to accentuate the incongruity of the assembly, there stood at the head a few smartly dressed men, sporting expensive ties.

"Them is big shots," Leo thought to himself. "Them ain't stevedores."

Then the ungainly crowd began to move, and Leo found himself involuntarily moving with them. The indistinct babbling ceased. Placards rose high in the air and voices shouted to the heavens.

Starting at first in the front, the song swiftly spread through the assembly like a summer fire in a dense forest.

"Sing, comrade, sing," a burly bare-foot picket commanded Leo, shoving him against the back of a formidable looking *marchande*.[7]

The street reverberated with the shuffling of their steps and the sound of their voices, as bass blended with soprano into one soul-gripping symphony.

[7]*marchande*: market woman.

Hold the fort for we are coming
Union men be strong

The words which came rapidly to Leo found a dim echo deep within his breast which, as he marched and sang, rose to a choking crescendo.

He stumbled out of the demonstration and stood at the corner of Prince and Henry Streets in order to catch his breath. Many persons were standing on the pavements and one of these he heard comment to another, "If they would only maintain this solidarity, they'll surely win."

Leo turned round and noticed that the speaker was a tall, neatly dressed, bespectacled youth with a tuft of beard concealing his chin. For a moment Leo's eyes were imprisoned by the glare of the young man's shining pair of shoes; and he could not resist a cynical chuckle as he looked at his own dirty, red-spotted alpargatas[8] through whose narrow mouths his unwashed toes protruded.

Leo's soul became emeshed in a disturbing emotional conflict. Thoughts of Mabel and her threat, of Eric and his remarks, of his own hunger, of the leaders of the demonstration, of the teachers, of the strike, and of his now unendurable and apparently purposeless existence were all, in some curious way, united in his brain.

He walked down Henry Street, away from the multitude, away from the contagious joy which reminded him of himself, away, away. Vaguely, as though through a mist, he saw and avoided the cars and carts which obstructed his route.

Eventually, he reached South Quay. A line of men were standing in front of a large, wooden building. Even this sight did not inspire him with hope. He was too weak. Yet he did not stop to ask any questions but drew instinctively closer to the line.

"Psst, Leo!" came a hoarse, familiar whisper. "Look, a room in here!"

Spinning round, his face flushed for a moment, Leo hesitated. He turned to leave. But before he could move, Eric's long hand had gripped him.

"Come, you young fool, come in here before you lose your chance," Eric said.

For one deep, significant moment, Leo resisted Eric's tugging.

---

[8]*alpargatus*: Casual footwear. Heelless, open-toed sandals with woven corded uppers and leather soles.

He seemed totally paralysed as his contradictory thoughts revolved in one maddening, ever-narrowing circle. He felt them racing to a challenging climax. And when it came, he chose.

Squeezing himself behind Eric, he hardly heard the latter covetously[9] whisper to him, "Is three dollars a day the Government giving we! Black people too damn foolish!"

"Uh-huh!" was Leo's laconic[10] reply.

[9]*covetously*: enviously.
[10]*laconic*: brief and non-committal.

My Fathers Before Me

Karl Sealy *(Barbados)*

Dick, the yard man, took the big Rhode Island cock from the run and, tucking it under his arm, went back to the kitchen steps where he had been sitting.

He held the cock fast between his legs and, squeezing its mouth open with his left hand, took a pinch of ashes from the small heap beside him, between right thumb and forefinger. This he rubbed on to the bird's tongue, and began to peel the hard, horny growth from the tongue's end.

His grandmother, who had spent most of her usefulness with the family, came shambling from the house behind him, eating cassava farina soaked in water and sugar. She stood looking down at him for some time, her eyes, the colour of dry bracken, tender, before she took a spoonful of farina from the glass and, bending with the stiffness of years, put it from behind into his mouth. Through the farina in his mouth Dick said, like a man continuing his thought in speech:

"And your age, Granny? You've spent a lifetime here. How many summers have you seen?"

"More than you'll ever see if you go to England," she said, letting herself down on the step above him. "Eighty-four years come October, God spare life. Whole fourteen above-and-beyond what the good Lord says."

"Hmm," Dick said, and taking the cock to the run, returned with a hen as white as a swan.

The old woman said: "Just think of it, Dick, just think of it. Come this time tomorrow you'll be miles away, with oceans of water separating you from everybody who loves you, and going to a land where you ent got a bird in the cotton tree, where nobody'll care a straw whether you sink or swim, and where black ent altogether liked." She scraped the last of the farina from the glass, and once more put the spoon to his mouth.

"You ent mind leaving us, Dick?" she said. "You ent mind leaving your poor old Granny and Ma? And Vere? What about Vere? You ent got no feelings in that belly of ye'n, Dick?"

Sucking farina from his teeth with his tongue, Dick said: "I'll

80

send for Vere as soon as I can. Maybe Ma, too."

The old woman continued as though she had not heard: "No more Dick about the house to put your hands 'pon. Maybe some lazy wringneck governor in your place whose only interest'll be his week's pay."

"Time enough too, and welcome," Dick said.

From an upstairs window, whose curtains she had been pulling against the evening sun, Bessie saw her mother sitting on the concrete step above Dick. Going down to the servants' room she took a cushion from the sofa and went out to where they were sitting. She said:

"Up, Ma. Think you're young, sitting on this cold step?"

The old woman raised herself a few inches, and Bessie pushed the cushion under her.

"I's just been telling Dick, Bessie, how no good ent ever come to our family leaving our land and going into nobody else country."

"True enough," said Bessie. "Look at my Dick and Panama."

Then the old woman asked: "Ever teach you who the Boers was at school, Dick?"

"I ent ever learn for sure who the Boers were," said Dick, "save that they couldn't stand up to bayonets."

"That's right," Bessie said. " 'At the bayonet charge the Boers surrender.' "

"British bayonets," Dick remarked.

"Don't you let nobody fool you with that, Dick," said the old woman. "There wasn't all no British bayonets. Your gran'dad's bayonet was there, too."

"Oh, well, we're all British. At least that's the way I look at it."

"But British or no British," said the old woman, "your gran'-dad came back to me and his four children with a foot less, and as I often told him after, it served him in a way right. For what in the name of heaven had the Boers ever done him, whoever in God's name they was, that he should leave off peaceful shoeing horses, and go in their own country to fight them for it? What right he had, Dick, answer that question, nuh?"

Dick, having peeled the pip off the hen's tongue, handed the bird up to Bessie, who laid it in her lap and began to stroke its feathers.

"Didn't it serve him in a way right, don't you think, Dick?" the old woman insisted. "Going to kill those Boers who'd never done him a single thing? Speak from your conscience, Dick."

Dick said, turning the bit of callus from the hen's tongue round his fingertips: "Well, he went to fight for his kind. To defend the Empire."

"The Empire?"

"The Empire," Dick said.

"What Empire?"

"The British Empire!"

"Listen, Dick," said the old woman. "I can't ever get this straight though I must have tried dozens of times to get the old man to put it right in my brain before he died: Ent Britain England?"

"Sure. Britain is England," said Dick.

"And ent British come from Britain?"

Dick said, perhaps not too sure of himself: "Well ... yes. British from Britain."

"And how come that your gran'dad lost his leg at a place called Mother River in Africa, as he was so fond of relating, and you says that he went to fight for the king of England? What right had the king of England in Africa?"

"Well, I don't think that the king of England was there in person," said Dick. "But he had, well ... interests there."

"Interests?" said the old woman.

"Well, it's like this," said Dick. "Years ago, just as we from the West Indies are going to England now, English men and women, British if you like, went and made their homes in other lands, Canada——"

"That's where Vere's sister gone to a hotel to do waitressing," interrupted Bessie.

"... Australia, Africa, and so on," continued Dick. "And these places where the British made their homes became British and made up the British Empire. So the king of England had a right to interfere if any other nation tried to pinch the places where these English had made their homes, as the Boers wanted to do."

"Oh, I see," said the old woman, shaking her head up and down. "It's a little bit clearer now than I's ever understood it before. But how come you's all flocking to England like a parcel of sheep? Why don't some of you go to Australia or Canada? Sure, Vere says she gets sixty-seven cents on every dollar that her sister sends her. Why don't some of you try and work for Canadian dollars to send back home? Ent you just told me we's all British?"

Dick said: "Well, it's like this: A man had, say, twelve children. As the years passed by, the oldest grew up and left the old man and went and made their own homes. Mind you, you couldn't interfere with the old man and the younger kids they'd left at home for them to know, but at the same time the old man couldn't tell them who to let come in their houses and who not to. Well, it's like that with Canada and Australia and South Africa. They have grown up and are running their own homes, and they say they don't want us West Indians to come into them and that's the end of it."

"But we can still run about in the backyard of the old home," said the old woman. "Is that what you mean?"

"Exactly. If you put it that way."

"I see it all now. I see. Your gran'dad was never given to explaining. Still, I don't feel that your gran'dad had any right going to fight those Boers," she persisted. "Just as I don't feel you've got any right leaving bright, sunny Barbados and going to that bleak England, though I's often thought that with your reading and quickness maybe you could do better than you're doing."

"I've thought so too, for a long time."

The evening sun had struck through the leaves into his eyes, and letting himself down upon the lowest step he sprawled back, making a rest for his head with his interlocked fingers. The women looked down on his face, and when he spoke his eyes had a faraway look into the sky.

Bessie said: "Your dad thought the same thing, and it didn't do him no good."

Vere, the young cook, appeared round the corner in the yard, carrying a basket of groceries in her hand.

She rested her basket on the ground and sat beside Dick with a sigh, leaning her body heavily upon him.

"Your dad thought Barbados was too slow for him too," said Bessie. "He swaggered about singing the foolish songs of the money they'd made digging the Canal with the other fools just like, as Ma says, our dad used to sing about the 'pound and a crown for every Boer they down'. Only he hadn't the luck that your gran'dad had. He didn't ever come back."

The old woman said: "Died like rotten sheep in the Panama mud. No, no good ent ever come to our family leaving our land and forking ourselves in nobody else's. Not one bit of good."

"Three for luck," Dick laughed.

Bessie got stiffly to her feet, walked over to the fowl run, and put the white fowl in. Then she came back and stood looking down at Vere.

"You's a foolish girl, Vere," said Bessie, after a time. "Why don't you tell this Dick not to go to England?"

" 'Cause it wouldn't be any use," said Vere.

"No use, nuh?" said the old woman. "Hm."

Vere said, sitting up and half-turning so that her words might be taken in by both women:

"You two had husbands, *husbands* mind you, and nothing you could say or do could stop them from going away once their minds was made up. I ent see how I's been more foolish than either of you 'cause I ent been able to stop Dick here from going."

Dick executed a long stretch before he said: "My grandfather was sick of cleaning up the mess that Miss Barbara's dogs made in the morning, sick of watering the gardens under the big evergreen, sick of cleaning pips off these stupid fowls, sick of waiting for the few paltry shillings at the end of the week, just as heartily sick of the whole deuced show as I am myself now.

"And so when the chance of going to Panama came along nothing nobody could say could stop him from going, just as nothing nobody can say will stop me from going to England. My grandfather and dad didn't go because they were foolish, but because they were brave. They didn't go because they wanted to be rid of their wives and children. They didn't go because they wanted an easy life. They didn't go for a spree. They went because their souls cried out for better opportunities and better breaks. And just like them, I'm going for the same thing."

Bessie was still standing there her hands akimbo, looking down at Dick. When Dick finished speaking her eyes switched their measure to Vere, and with a fleeting lightening of her harsh face which none of the others saw she decided to play her last card.

"Still, Vere," said Bessie, "you're a foolish girl."

Vere pouted: "Say it again. A hundred times. Till you're tired."

"What're you straightening your hair so for?" Bessie asked.

" 'Cause other girls do," said Vere.

"And rouging your face, and plastering that red thing on to your mouth?"

" 'Cause other girls do." Vere hugged her knees, rocking herself back and forth on the step.

"You was always a rude brazen little girl. All the same, I hope you's got something else to make Dick stick by you. He going to England where he'll see hundreds of girls with real straight hair and really red cheeks and mouths natural like roses. Ten to one, one of them will get him."

Vere sprang to her feet, her eyes dilated.

"And I'd spend the last cent getting to England, and wherever they was I'd find them out and tear the last straight hair from her head. I'd tear the flesh from her red cheeks to the bone!

"I'd beat her rosy mouth to a bloody pulp! Oh Christ, I'd . . ."

She caught at her breath in a long racking sob, snatched the basket from the ground and ran into the house.

The other three were all standing now, and in the understanding of Vere's love, had drawn involuntarily closer to one another.

The old woman said, knocking a beetle from Dick's shirt with her spoon: "And will you still go to England, Dick?"

Their ears just barely caught the one word from his lips.

The women turned and, mounting the steps in the settling dusk, made their way together into the house.

The old woman said: "It's the same with him as it was with them, Bessie. Nothing will ever stop him."

"No. Nothing," said Bessie.

Cane is Bitter

Samuel Selvon *(Trinidad)*

In February they began to reap the cane[1] in the undulating[2] fields at Cross Crossing estate in the southern part of Trinidad. "Crop time coming boy, plenty work for everybody," men in the village told one another. They set about sharpening their cutlasses on grinding stones, ceasing only when they tested the blades with their thumb-nails and a faint ping! quivered in the air. Or they swung the cutlass at a drooping leaf and cleaved it. But the best test was when it could shave the hairs off your leg.

Everyone was happy in Cross Crossing as work loomed up in the way of their idleness, for after the planting of the cane there was hardly any work until the crop season. They laughed and talked more and the children were given more liberty than usual, so they ran about the barracks and played hide and seek in those canefields which had not yet been fired to make the reaping easier. In the evening, when the dry trash was burnt away from the stalks of sweet juice, they ran about clutching the black straw which rose on the wind: people miles away knew when crop season was on for the burnt trash was blown a great distance away. The children smeared one another on the face and laughed at the black streaks. It wouldn't matter now if their exertions made them hungry, there would be money to buy flour and rice when the men worked in the fields, cutting and carting the cane to the weighing-bridge.

In a muddy pond about two hundred yards east of the settlement, under the shade of spreading *laginette* trees, women washed clothes and men bathed mules and donkeys and hog-cattle. The women beat the clothes with stones to get them clean, squatting by the banks, their skirts drawn tight against the back of their thighs, their saris retaining grace of arrangement on their shoulders even in that awkward position. Naked children splashed about in the pond, hitting the water with their hands and shouting when the water shot up in the air at different angles, and

---

[1] *cane*: sugar cane, one of the main crops in Trinidad.

[2] *undulating*: gently moving like waves, as corn does in wind.

trying to make brief rainbows in the sunlight with the spray. Rays of the morning sun came slantways from halfway up in the sky, casting the shadow of trees on the pond, and playing on the brown bodies of the children.

Ramlal came to the pond and sat on the western bank, so that he squinted into the sunlight. He dipped his cutlass in the water and began to sharpen it on the end of a rock on which his wife Rookmin was beating clothes. He was a big man, and in earlier days was reckoned handsome. But work in the fields had not only tanned his skin to a deep brown but actually changed his features. His nose had a slight hump just above the nostrils, and the squint in his eyes was there even in the night, as if he was peering all the time, though his eyesight was remarkable. His teeth were stained brown with tobacco, so brown that when he laughed it blended with the colour of his face, and you only saw the lips stretched wide and heard the rumble in his throat.

Rookmin was frail but strong as most East Indian women.[3] She was not beautiful, but it was difficult to take any one feature of her face and say it was ugly. Though she was only thirty-six, hard work and the bearing of five children had taken toll. Her eyes were black and deceptive, and perhaps she might have been unfaithful to Ramlal if the idea had ever occurred to her. But like most of the Indians in the country districts, half her desires and emotions were never given a chance to live, her life dedicated to wresting an existence for herself and her family. But as if she knew the light she threw from her eyes, she had a habit of shutting them whenever she was emotional. Her breasts sagged from years of suckling. Her hands were wrinkled and callous. The toes of her feet were spread wide from walking without any footwear whatsoever: she never had need for a pair of shoes because she never left the village.

She watched Ramlal out of the corner of her eye as he sharpened the cutlass, sliding the blade to and fro on the rock. She knew he had something on his mind, the way how he had come silently and sat near to her pretending that he could add to the keenness of his razor-sharp cutlass. She waited for him to speak, in an oriental respectfulness. But from the attitude of both of them, it wasn't possible to tell that they were about to

[3] *East Indian women*: that is, a descendant of those who came from the East Indies to work in the Caribbean.

converse, or even that they were man and wife. Rookmin went on washing clothes, turning the garments over and over as she pounded them on a flat stone, and Ramlal squinted his eyes and looked at the sun.

At last, after five minutes or so, Ramlal spoke.

"Well, that boy Romesh coming home tomorrow. Is six months since last he come home. This time, I make up my mind, he not going back."

Rookmin went on scrubbing, she did not even look up.

"You see how city life change the boy. When he was here the last time, you see how he was talking about funny things?"

Rookmin held up a tattered white shirt and looked at the sun through it.

"But you think he will agree to what we going to do?" she asked. "He must be learning all sorts of new things, and this time might be worse than last time. Suppose he want to take creole wife?"

"But you mad or what? That could never happen. Ain't we make all arrangement with Sampath for Doolsie to married him? Anyway," he went on, "is all your damn fault in the first place, wanting to send him for education in the city. You see what it cause? The boy come like a stranger as soon as he start to learn all those funny things they teach you in school, talking about poetry and books and them funny things. I did never want to send him for education, but is you who make me do it."

"Education is a good thing," Rookmin said, without intonation. "One day he might come lawyer or doctor, and all of we would live in a big house in the town, and have servants to look after we."

"That is only foolish talk," Ramlal said. "You think he would remember we when he come a big man? And besides, by that time you and me both dead. And besides, the wedding done plan and everything already."

"Well, if he married Doolsie everything might work out."

"How you mean if? I had enough of all this business. He have to do what I say, else I put him out and he never come here again. Doolsie father offering big dowry, and afterwards the both of them could settle on the estate and he could forget all that business."

Rookmin was silent. Ramlal kept testing the blade with his nail, as if he were fascinated by the pinging sound, as if he were trying to pick out a tune.

But in fact he was thinking, thinking about the last time his son Romesh had come home . . .

It was only his brothers and sisters, all younger than himself, who looked at Romesh with wonder, wanting to ask him questions about the world outside the canefields and the village. Their eyes expressed their thoughts, but out of some curious embarrassment they said nothing. In a way, this brother was a stranger, someone who lived far away in the city, only coming home once or twice a year to visit them. They were noticing a change, a distant look in his eyes. Silently, they drew aside from him, united in their lack of understanding. Though Romesh never spoke of the great things he was learning, or tried to show off his knowledge, the very way he bore himself now, the way he watched the cane moving in the wind was alien to their feelings. When they opened the books he had brought, eager to see the pictures, there were only pages and pages of words, and they couldn't read. They watched him in the night, crouching in the corner, the book on the floor near to the candle, reading. That alone made him different, set him apart. They thought he was going to be a pundit,[4] or a priest, or something extraordinary. Once his sister had asked: "What do you read so much about, *bhai*?" and Romesh looked at her with a strange look and said, "To tell you, you wouldn't understand. But have patience, a time will come soon, I hope, when all of you will learn to read and write." Then Hari, his brother, said, "Why do you feel we will not understand? What is wrong with our brains? Do you think because you go to school in the city that you are better than us? Because you get the best clothes to wear, and shoes to put on your feet, because you get favour from *bap* and *mai*?" Romesh said quickly, "*Bhai*, it is not that. It is only that I have left our village, and have learned about many things which you do not know about. The whole world goes ahead in all fields, in politics, in science, in art. Even now the governments in the West Indies are talking about federating the islands, and then what will happen to the Indians in this island? But we must not quarrel, soon all of us will have a chance." But Hari was not impressed. He turned to his father and mother and said: "See how he has changed. He don't want to play no games anymore, he don't want to work in the fields, he is too much of a bigshot to use a cutlass. His brothers and sisters are fools, he don't want to

[4]*pundit*: expert.

talk to them because they won't understand. He don't even want to eat we food again, this morning I see he ain't touch the *baghi*.[5] No. We have to get chicken for him, and the cream from all the cows in the village. Yes, that is what. And who it is does sweat for him to get pretty shirt to wear in Port of Spain?" He held up one of the girls' arms and spanned it with his fingers. "Look how thin she is. All that is for you to be a big man, and now you scorning your own family?" Romesh got up from the floor and faced them. His eyes burned fiercely, and he looked like the pictures of Indian gods the children had seen in the village hall. "You are all wrong!" he cried in a ringing voice, "surely you, *bap*, and you, *mai*, the years must have taught you that you must make a different life for your children, that you must free them from ignorance and the wasting away of their lives? Do you want them to suffer as you have?" Rookmin looked like she was going to say something, but instead she shut her eyes tight. Ramlal said: "Who tell you we suffer? We bring children in the world and we happy." But Romesh went on, "And what will the children do? Grow up in the village here, without learning to read and write? There are schools in San Fernando, surely you can send them there to learn about different things besides driving a mule and using a cutlass? Oh *bap*, we are such a backward people, all the others move forward to better lives, and we lag behind believing that what is to be, will be. All over Trinidad, in the country districts, our people toil on the land and reap the cane. For years it has been so, years in the same place, learning nothing new, accepting our fate like animals. Political men come from India and give speeches in the city. They speak of better things, they tell us to unite and strive for a greater goal. And what does it mean to you? Nothing. You are content to go hungry, to see your children run about naked, emaciated, grow up dull and stupid, slaves to your own indifference. You do not even pretend an interest in the Legislative Council. I remember why you voted for Pragsingh last year, it was because he gave you ten dollars – did I not see it for myself? It were better that we returned to India than stay in the West Indies and live such a low form of existence." The family watched Romesh wide-eyed. Ramlal sucked his clay pipe noisily. Rookmin held her youngest daughter in her lap, picking her head for lice, and now and then shutting her eyes so the others wouldn't see what she was thinking. "There is only one

[5] *baghi*: a type of spinach which is generally fried with onions or garlic.

solution," Romesh went on, "we must educate the children, open up new worlds in their minds, stretch the horizon of their thoughts ..." Suddenly he stopped. He realised that for some time now they weren't listening, his words didn't make any sense to them. Perhaps he was going about this the wrong way, he would have to find some other way of explaining how he felt. And was he sufficiently equipped in himself to propose vast changes in the lives of the people? It seemed to him then how small he was, how there were so many things he didn't know. All the books he'd read, the knowledge he'd lapped up hungrily in the city, listening to the politicians making speeches in the square – all these he mustered to his assistance. But it was as if his brain was too small, it was like putting your mouth in the sea and trying to drink all the water. Wearily, like an old man who had tried to prove his point merely by repeating, "I am old, I should know," Romesh sat down on the floor, and there was silence in the hut, a great silence, as if the words he'd spoken had fled the place and gone outside with the wind and the cane.

And so after he had gone back to the city his parents discussed the boy, and concluded that the only thing to save his senses was to marry him off. "You know he like Sampath daughter from long time, and she is a hard-working girl, she go make good wife for him," Rookmin had said. Ramlal had seen Sampath and everything was fixed. Everybody in the willage knew of the impending wedding ...

Romesh came home the next day. He had some magazines and books under his arm, and a suitcase in his hand. There was no reception for him; everyone who could work was out in the fields.

He was as tall as the canes on either side of the path on which he walked. He sniffed the smell of burning cane, but he wasn't overjoyful at coming home. He had prepared for this, prepared for the land on which he had toiled as a child, the thatched huts, the children running naked in the sun. He knew that these were things not easily forgotten which he had to forget. But he saw how waves of wind rippled over the seas of cane and he wondered vaguely about big things like happiness and love and poetry, and how they could fit into the poor, toiling lives the villagers led.

Romesh met his sisters at home. They greeted him shyly but he held them in his arms and cried, "*Beti*, do you not know your own brother?" And they laughed and hung their heads on his shoulder.

Everybody gone to work," one girl said, "and we cooking food to carry. Pa and Ma was looking out since early this morning, they say to tell you if come to come in the fields."

Romesh looked around the hut in which he had grown up. It seemed to him that if he had come back home after ten years, there would still be the old table in the centre of the room, its feet sunk in the earthen floor, the black pots and pans hanging on nails near the window. Nothing would change. They would plant the cane, and when it grew and filled with sweet juice cut it down for the factory. The children would waste away their lives working with their parents. No schooling, no education, no widening of experience. It was the same thing the man had lectured about in the public library three nights before in Port of Spain. The most they would learn would be to weild a cutlass expertly, or drive the mule cart to the railway line swiftly so that before the sun went down they would have worked sufficiently to earn more than their neighbours.

With a sigh like an aged man Romesh opened his suitcase and took out a pair of shorts and a polo shirt. He put these on and put the suitcase away in a corner. He wondered where would be a safe place to put his books. He opened the suitcase again and put them in.

It was as if, seeing the room in which he had argued and quarrelled with the family on his last visit, he lost any happiness he might have had coming back this time. A feeling of depression overcame him.

It lasted as he talked with his sisters as they prepared food to take to the fields. Romesh listened how they stumbled with words, how they found it difficult to express themselves. He thought how regretful it was that they couldn't go to school. He widened the thought and embraced all the children in the village, growing up with such little care, running naked in the mud with a piece of *roti*[6] in their hands, missing out on all the things that life should stand for.

But when the food was ready and they set off for the fields, with the sun in their eyes making them blind, he felt better. He would try to be happy with them, while he was here. No more preaching. No more voicing of opinion on this or that.

Other girls joined his sisters as they walked, all carrying food. When they saw Romesh they blushed and tittered, and he

[6]*roti*: a kind of bread, eaten especially with savoury foods.

wondered what they were whispering about among themselves.

There were no effusive greetings. Sweating as they were, their clothes black with the soot of burnt canes, their bodies caught in the motions of their work, they just shouted out, and Romesh shouted back. Then Ramlal dropped the reins and jumped down from his cart. He curved his hand like a boomerang and swept it over his face. The soot from his sleeves smeared his face as he wiped away the sweat.

Rookmin came up and opened tired arms to Romesh. "*Beta*," she cried as she felt his strong head on her breast. She would have liked to stay like that, drawing his strength and vitality into her weakened body, and closing her eyes so her emotions wouldn't show.

"*Beta*," his father said, "you getting big, you looking strong." They sat down to eat on the grass. Romesh was the only one who appeared cool, the others were flushed, the veins standing out on their foreheads and arms.

Romesh asked if it was a good crop.

"Yes *beta*," Ramlal said, "is a good crop, and plenty work for everybody. But this year harder than last year, because rain begin to fall early, and if we don't hurry up with the work, it will be too much trouble for all of us. The overseer come yesterday, and he say a big bonus for the man who do the most work. So everybody working hard for that bonus. Two of my mules sick, but I have to work them, I can't help. We trying to get the bonus."

After eating Ramlal fished a cigarette zoot from his pocket and lit it carefully. First greetings over, he had nothing more to tell his son, for the time being anyway.

Romesh knew they were all remembering the last visit, and the things he had said then. This time he wasn't going to say anything, he was just going to have a holiday and enjoy it, and return to school in the city refreshed.

He said, "Hari, I bet I could cut more canes than you."

Hari laughed. "Even though I work the whole morning already is a good bet. You must be forget to use *poya*,[7] your hands so soft and white now."

That is the way life is, Ramlal thought as Romesh took his cutlass. Education, school, chut! It was only work put a *roti* in your belly, only work that brought money. The marriage would change Romesh. And he felt a pride in his heart as his son spat

[7]*poya*: a special kind of baghi (see page 90), often known as "English spinach".

on the blade.

The young men went to a patch of burnt canes. The girls came too, standing by to pile the fallen stalks of sweet juice into heaps, so that they could be loaded quickly and easily on to the carts and raced to the weighing-bridge.

Cane fell as if a machine were at work. The blades swung in the air, glistened for a moment in the sunlight, and descended on the stalks near the roots. Though the work had been started as a test of speed, neither of them moved ahead of the other. Sometimes Romesh paused until Hari came abreast, and sometimes Hari waited a few canes for Romesh. Once they looked at each other and laughed, the sweat on their faces getting into their mouths. There was no more enmity on Hari's part: seeing his brother like this, working, was like the old days when they worked side by side at all the chores which filled the day.

Everybody turned to in the field striving to outwork the others, for each wanted the bonus as desperately as his neighbour. Sometimes the women and the girls laughed or made jokes to one another, but the men worked silently. And the crane on the weighing-bridge creaked and took load after load. The labourer manipulating it grumbled: there was no bonus for him, though his wage was more than that of the cane-cutters.

When the sun set all stopped work as if by signal. And in Ramlal's hut that night there was laughter and song. Everything was all right, they thought. Romesh was his natural self again, the way he swung that cutlass! His younger sisters and brother had never really held anything against him, and now that Hari seemed pleased, they dropped all embarrassment and made fun. "See *bhai*, I make *meetai* especially for you," his sister said, offering the sweetmeat.

"He work hard, he deserve it," Hari agreed, and he looked at his brother almost with admiration.

Afterwards, when Ramlal was smoking and Rookmin was searching in the youngest girl's head for lice ("put pitch-oil, that will kill them," Ramlal advised) Romesh said he was going to pay Doolsie a visit.

There was a sudden silence. Rookmin shut her eyes, the children, stopped playing, and Ramlal coughed over his pipe.

"Well, what is the matter?" Romesh asked, looking at their faces.

"Well, now," Ramlal began, and stopped to clear his throat. "Well now, you know that is our custom, that a man shouldn't go to pay visit to the girl he getting married . . ."

"What!" Romesh looked from face to face. The children shuffled their feet and began to be embarrassed at the stranger's presence once more.

Ramlal spoke angrily. "Remember that is your father's house! Remember the smaller ones! Careful what you say, you must give respect! You not expect to get married one day, eh? Is a good match we make, boy, you will get good dowry, and you could live in the village and forget them funny things you learning in the city."

"So it has all been arranged," Romesh said slowly. "That is why everybody looked at me in such a strange way in the fields. My life already planned for me, my path pointed out – cane, labour, boy children, and the familiar village of Cross Crossing." His voice had dropped lower, as if he had been speaking to himself, but it rose again as he addressed his mother: "And you, *mai*, you have helped them do this to me? You whose idea it was to give me an education?"

Rookmin shut her eyes and spoke. "Is the way of our people, is we custom from long time. And you is Indian? The city fool your brains, but you will get back accustom after you married and have children."

Ramlal got up from where he was squatting on the floor, and faced Romesh. "You have to do what we say," he said loudly. "Ever since you in the city, we notice how you change. You forgetting custom and how we Indian people does live. And too besides, money getting short. We want help on the estate. The garden want attention, and nobody here to see about the cattle and them. And no work after crop, too besides."

"Then I can go to school in San Fernando," Romesh said desperately. "If there is no money to pay the bus, I will walk. The government schools are free, you do not have to pay to learn."

"You will married and have boy children," Ramlal said, "and you will stop answering your *bap* . . ."

"Hai! Hai!" Drivers urged their carts in the morning sun, and whips cracked crisply on the air. Dew still clung to the grass as workers took to the fields to do as much as they could before the heat of the sun began to tell.

Romesh was still asleep when the others left. No one woke him; they moved about the hut in silence. No one spoke. The boys went to harness the mules, one of the girls to milk the cows and the other was busy in the kitchen.

When Romesh got up he opened his eyes in full awareness. He could have started the argument again as if no time had elapsed, the night had made no difference.

He went into the kitchen to wash his face. He gargled noisily, scraped his tongue with his teeth. Then he remembered his toothbrush and toothpaste in his suitcase. As he cleaned his teeth his sister stood watching him. She never used a toothbrush: they broke a twig and chewed it to clean their mouths.

"You going to go away, *bhai*?" she asked him timidly.

He nodded, with froth in his mouth.

"If you stay, you could teach we what you know," the girl said.

Romesh washed his mouth and said, "*Baihin*, there are many things I have yet to learn."

"But what will happen to us?"

"Don't ask me questions, little sister," he said crossly.

After he had eaten he left the hut and sulked about the village, walking slowly with his hands in his pockets. He wasn't quite sure what he was going to do. He kept telling himself that he would go away and never return, but bonds he had refused to think about surrounded him. The smell of burnt cane was strong on the wind. He went to the pond, where he and Hari used to bath the mules. What to do? His mind was in a turmoil.

Suddenly he turned and went home. He got his cutlass – it was sharp and clean, even though unused for such a long time. Ramlal never allowed any of his tools to get rusty.

He went out into the fields, swinging the cutlass in the air, as if with each stroke he swept a problem away.

Hari said: "Is time you come. Other people start work long time, we have to work extra to catch up with them."

There was no friendliness in his voice now.

Romesh said nothing, but he hacked savagely at the canes, and in half an hour he was bathed in sweat and his skin scratched from contact with the cane.

Ramlal came up in the mule cart and called out, "Work faster! We a whole cartload behind!" Then he saw Romesh and he came down from the cart and walked rapidly across. "So you come! Is a good thing you make up your mind!"

Romesh wiped his face. "I am not going to stay, *bap*." It was funny how the decision came, he hadn't known himself what he was going to do. "I will help with the crop, you shall get the bonus if I have to work alone in the night. But I am not going to get married. I am going away after the crop."

"You are mad, you will do as I say." Ramlal spoke loudly, and other workers in the field stopped to listen.

The decision was so clear in Romesh's mind that he did not say anything more. He swung the cutlass tirelessly at the cane and knew that when the crop was finished, it would be time to leave his family and the village. His mind got that far, and he didn't worry about after that ...

As the wind whispered in the cane, it carried the news of Romesh's revolt against his parents' wishes, against tradition and custom.

Doolsie, working a short distance away, turned her brown face from the wind. But women and girls working near to her whispered among themselves and laughed. Then one of the bolder women, already married, said, "Well girl, is a good thing in a way. Some of these men too bad. They does beat their wife too much – look at Dulcie husband, he does be drunk all the time, and she does catch hell with him."

But Doolsie bundled the canes together and kept silent.

"She too young yet," another said. "Look, she breasts not even form yet!"

Doolsie did not have any memories to share with Romesh, and her mind was young enough to bend under any weight. But the way her friends were laughing made her angry, and in her mind she too revolted against the marriage.

"All-you too stupid!" she said, lifting her head with a childish pride so that her sari fell on her shoulder. "You wouldn't say Romesh is the only boy in the village! And too besides, I wasn't going to married him if he think he too great for me."

The wind rustled through the cane. Overhead, the sun burned like a furnace.

A Drink of Water

Samuel Selvon *(Trinidad)*

The time when the rains didn't come for three months and the sun was a yellow furnace in the sky was known as the Great Drought in Trinidad. It happened when everyone was expecting the sky to burst open with rain to fill the dry streams and water the parched earth.

But each day was the same; the sun rose early in a blue sky, and all day long the farmers lifted their eyes, wondering what had happened to Parjanya, the rain god. They rested on their hoes and forks and wrung perspiration from their clothes, seeing no hope in labour, terrified by the thought that if no rain fell soon they would lose their crops and livestock and face starvation and death.

In the tiny village of Las Lomas, out in his vegetable garden, Manko licked dry lips and passed a wet sleeve over his dripping face. Somewhere in the field a cow mooed mournfully, sniffing around for a bit of green in the cracked earth. The field was a desolation of drought. The trees were naked and barks peeled off trunks as if they were diseased. When the wind blew, it was heavy and unrelieving, as if the heat had taken all the spirit out of it. But Manko still opened his shirt and turned his chest to it when it passed.

He was a big man, grown brown and burnt from years of working on the land. His arms were bent and he had a crouching position even when he stood upright. When he laughed he showed more tobacco stain than teeth.

But Manko had not laughed for a long time. Bush fires had swept Las Lomas and left the garden plots charred and smoking. Cattle were dropping dead in the heat. There was scarcely any water in the village; the river was dry with scummy mud. But with patience one could collect a bucket of water. Boiled, with a little sugar to make it drinkable, it had to do.

Sometimes, when the children knew that someone had gone to the river for water, they hung about in the village main road waiting with bottles and calabash shells, and they fell upon the water-carrier as soon as he hove in sight.

"Boil the water first before drinking!" was the warning cry. But even so two children were dead and many more were on the sick list, their parents too poor to seek medical aid in the city twenty miles away.

Manko sat in the shade of a mango tree and tried to look on the bright side of things. Such a dry season meant that the land would be good for corn seeds when the rains came. He and his wife Rannie had been working hard and saving money with the hope of sending Sunny, their son, to college in the city.

Rannie told Manko: "We poor, and we ain't have no education, but is all right, we go get old soon and dead, and what we have to think about is the boy. We must let him have plenty learning and come a big man in Trinidad."

And Manko, proud of his son, used to boast in the evening, when the villagers got together to talk and smoke, that one day Sunny would be a lawyer or a doctor.

But optimism was difficult now. His livestock was dying out, and the market was glutted with yams. He had a great pile in the yard which he could not sell.

Manko took a look at his plot of land and shook his head. There was no sense in working any more today. He took his cutlass and hoe and calabash shell which had a string so he could hold it dangling. He shook it, and realised with burning in his throat that it was empty, though he had left a few mouthfuls in it. He was a fool; he should have known that the heat would dry it up if he took it out in the garden with him. He licked his lips and, shouldering the tools, walked slowly down the winding path which led to his hut.

Rannie was cooking in the open fireplace in the yard. Sunny was sitting under the poui tree, but when he saw his father he ran towards him and held the calabash shell eagerly. Always when Manko returned from the fields he brought back a little water for his son. But this time he could only shake his head.

"Who went for water today by the river?" he asked Rannie.

"I think was Jagroop," she answered, stirring the pot with a large wooden spoon, "but he ain't coming back till late."

She covered the pot and turned to him. "Tomorrow we going to make offering for rain," she said.

Next day, Las Lomas held a big feast, and prayers were said to the rain god, Parjanya. And then two days later, a man called Rampersad struck water in a well he had been digging for weeks. It was the miracle they had been praying for. That day everyone

99

drank their fill, and Rampersad allowed each villager a bucket of water, and Manko told Sunny: 'See how blessing doesn't only come from up the sky, it does come from the earth, too."

Rampersad's wife was a selfish and crafty woman, and while the villagers were filling their buckets she stood by the doorway of their hut and watched them. That night she told her husband he was a fool to let them have the water for nothing.

"They have money hide up," she urged him. "They could well pay for it. The best thing to do is to put barb' wire all round the well, and set a watchdog to keep guard in the night so nobody thief the water. Then say you too poor to give away for nothing. Charge a dollar for a bucket and two shillings for half-bucket. We make plenty money and come rich."

When Rampersad announced this, the villagers were silent and aghast that a man could think of such a scheme when the whole village was burning away in the drought, and two children had died.

Rampersad bought a shotgun and said he would shoot anyone he found trespassing on his property. He put up the barbed wire and left a ferocious watchdog near the well at nights.

As April went, there was still no sign in the sky. In Las Lomas, the villagers exhausted their savings in buying Rampersad's water to keep alive.

Manko got up one morning and looked in the tin under his bed in which he kept his money. There was enough for just two buckets of water. He said to Rannie: "How long could you make two buckets of water last, if we use it only for drinking?"

"That is all the money remaining?" Rannie looked at him with fear.

He nodded and looked outside where the poui tree had begun to blossom. "Is a long time now," he said softly, "a long time, too long. It can't last. The rain will fall, just don't be impatient."

Rannie was not impatient, but thirst made her careless. It happened soon after the two buckets were empty. She forgot to boil a pan of river water, and only after she had drunk a cupful did she realise her fatal mistake. She was afraid to tell Manko; she kept silent about the incident.

Next day, she could not get out of bed. She rolled and tossed as fever ravaged her body.

Manko's eyes were wide with fright when he saw the signs of fever. Sunny, who had not been to school for weeks, wanted to do whatever he could, anything at all, to get his mother well so she could talk and laugh and cook again.

He spoke to his father after Rannie had fallen into a fitful sleep, with perspiration soaking through the thin white sheet.

"No money remaining for water, *bap*?"

Manko shook his head.

"And no money for doctor or medicine?"

He shook his head again.

"But how it is this man Rampersad have so much water and we ain't have any? Why don't we just go and take it?"

"The water belong to Rampersad," Manko said. "Is his own, and if he choose to sell it, is his business. We can't just go and take, that would be thiefing. You must never thief from another man, Sunny. That is a big, big, sin. No matter what happen.

"But is not a fair thing." the boy protested, digging his hands into the brittle soil. "If we had clean water, we could get *mai* better, not so?"

"Yes, *beta*," Manko sighed and rose to his feet. "You stay and mind *mai*, I going to try and get some river water."

All day, Sunny sat in the hut brooding over the matter, trying hard to understand why his mother should die from lack of water when a well was filled in another man's yard.

It was late in the evening when Manko returned. As he had expected, the river was nearly dry, a foul trickle of mud not worth drinking. He found the boy quiet and moody. After a while, Sunny went out.

Manko was glad to be alone. He didn't want Sunny to see him leaving the hut later in the night, with the bucket and the rope. It would be difficult to explain that he was stealing Rampersad's water only because it was a matter of life or death.

He waited impatiently for Rannie to fall asleep. It seemed she would never close her eyes. She just turned and twisted restlessly, and once she looked at him and asked if rain had fallen, and he put his rough hand on her hot forehead and said softly no, but that he had seen a sign that evening, a great black cloud low down in the east.

Then suddenly her fever rose again, and she was delirious. This time he could not understand what she said. She was moaning in a queer, strangled way.

It was midnight before she fell into a kind of swoon, a red flush on her face. Manko knew what he must do now. He stood looking at her, torn between the fear of leaving her and the desperate plan that he had made. She might die while he was gone, and yet – he must try it.

He frowned as he went out and saw the moon like a night sun in the sky, lighting up the village. He turned to the east and his heart leapt as he saw the cloud moving towards the village in a slow breeze. It seemed so far away, and it was moving as if it would take days to get over the fields. Perhaps it would; perhaps it would change direction and go scudding down into the west, and not a drop of water.

He moved off towards the well, keeping behind the huts and deep into the trees. It took him ten minutes to get near the barbed wire fence, and he stood in the shadow of a giant silk-cotton tree. He leaned against the trunk and drew in his breath sharply as his eyes discerned a figure on the other side of the well, outside the barbed wire.

The figure stopped, as though listening, then began clambering over the fence.

Even as he peered to see if he could recognise who it was, a sudden darkness fell as the cloud swept over the moon in the freshening wind.

Manko cast his eyes upwards swiftly, and when he looked down again the figure was on the brink of the well, away from the sleeping watchdog.

It was a great risk to take; it was the risk Manko himself had to take. But this intrusion upset his plan. He could not call out; the slightest sound would wake the dog, and what it did not do to the thief, Rampersad would do with his shotgun.

For a moment, Manko's heart failed him. He smelt death very near – for the unknown figure at the well, and for himself, too. He had been a fool to come. Then a new frenzy seized him. He remembered the cruel red flush on Rannie's cheeks when he had left her. Let her die happy, if a drop of water could make her so. Let her live, if a drop of water could save her. His own thirst flared in his throat; how much more she must be suffering!

He saw the bucket slide noiselessly down and the rope paid out. Just what he had planned to do. Now draw it up, cautiously, yes, and put it to rest gently on the ground. Now kneel and take a drink, and put the fire out in your body. For God's sake, why didn't the man take a drink? What was he waiting for? Ah, that was it, but be careful, do not make the slightest noise, or everything will be ruined. Bend your head down . . .

Moonrays shot through a break in the cloud and lit up the scene.

It was Sunny.

"*Beta*!" Before he could think, the startled cry had left Manko's lips.

The dog sprang up at the sound and moved with uncanny swiftness. Before Sunny could turn, it had sprung across the well, straight at the boy's throat.

Manko scrambled over the fence, ripping away his clothes and drawing blood. He ran and cleared the well in a great jump, and tried to tear the beast away from the struggling boy. The dog turned, growling low in the throat as it faced this new attacker.

Manko stumbled and fell, breathing heavily. He felt teeth sink into his shoulder and he bit his lip hard to keep from screaming in pain.

Suddenly the dog was wrenched away as Sunny joined the fight. The boy put his arms around the dog's neck and jerked it away from his father with such force that when the animal let go they both fell rolling to the ground.

Manko flung out his arm as he sprang up. In doing so, he capsized the bucket of water with a loud clang. Even in the struggle for life he could not bear to see the earth sucking up the water like a sponge. In fear and fury, he snatched the empty bucket and brought it down with all his strength on the dog's head.

The animal gave a whimper and rolled off the boy and lay still.

"Who that, thiefing my water?" Rampersad came running out into the yard, firing his shotgun wildly in the air.

"Quick, boy! Over the fence!" Manko grabbed the bucket and tossed it over. He almost threw Sunny to safety as the boy faltered on the wire. Then he half-dragged his own bleeding body up, and fell exhausted on the other side.

Sunny put his arm under his father and helped him up. Together they ran into the shadow of the trees.

Ths noise of the gun and Rampersad's yells had wakened the whole village, and everyone was astir.

Father and son hid the bucket in a clump of dry bush and, waiting for a minute to recover themselves, joined the crowd which was gathering in front of Rampersad's hut.

Rampersad was beside himself with rage. He threatened them all with jail, screaming that he would find out who had stolen the water and killed the dog.

"Who is the thief? You catch him?" The crowd jeered and booed. "It damn good. Serve you right." Clutching his father's arm tightly, Sunny danced and chuckled with delight at Rampersad's discomfiture.

But suddenly silence and darkness fell together. A large black blob of cloud blotted out the moon. The sky was thick with clouds piling up on each other and there was a new coolness in the wind.

As one, the crowd knelt and prayed to the rain god. The sky grew black; it looked as if the moon had never been there. For hours they prayed, until Manko, thinking of Rannie, gently tapped his son and beckoned him away. They walked home hand in hand.

It was Sunny who felt the first drop. It lay on his hand like a diamond shining in the dark.

"*Bap*?" He raised questioning eyes to his father. "Look!"

As Manko looked up, another drop fell on his face and rolled down his cheek. The wind became stronger; there was a swift fall of some heavy drops. Then the wind died like a sigh. A low rumble in the east; then silence. Perhaps Parjanya was having a joke with them, perhaps there would be no rain after all.

And then it came sweeping in from the north-east, with a rising wind. Not very heavy at first, but in thrusts, coming and going. They opened their mouths and laughed, and water fell in. They shouted and cried and laughed again.

Manko approached the hut where Rannie lay, and he was trembling at what he would find. He said to the boy: "*Beta*. You stay here. I go in first to see *mai*." The boy's face went rigid with sudden fear. Though he was already drenched to the skin, he took shelter under the poui tree in the yard.

Manko was hardly inside the door when he gave a sharp cry of alarm. He thought he saw a ghostly figure tottering towards him, its face luminous-grey. He flattened himself against the wall and closed his eyes. It was cruel of the gods to torment him like this. This was not Rannie: Rannie was lying in bed in the next room, she could not be alive any more.

"Manko." It was her voice, and yet it was not her voice. "What noise is that I hear? Is rain?"

He could not speak. Slowly, he forced himself to stretch out his hand and touch her forehead. It felt cold and unnatural.

He withdrew his hand, and began to tremble uncontrollably.

"Manko," the lips formed the words. "Manko, give me water!"

Something fell to the floor with a clatter. He saw that it was a tin cup, and that she had been holding it in her hand. She swayed towards him, and he caught her. Then Manko knew that it was a miracle. Rannie was shaking with cold and weakness, but the fever was gone, and she was alive.

Realisation burst upon him with such force that he almost fainted.

He muttered: "I will get some for you."

He picked up the cup and ran out into the lashing rain. Sunny, watching from the poui tree, was astonished to see his father standing motionless in the downpour. He had taken off his shirt, and his bare back and chest were shining with water. His face, uplifted to the sky, was the face of a man half-crazy with joy. He might be laughing or crying, Sunny could not tell; and his cheeks were streaming, perhaps with tears, perhaps with Parjanya's rain.

Shark Fins

Enrique Serpa *(Cuba)*

Felip had the strange feeling that the sound of the alarm clock was following like a large fish through the waters of sleep. Still not fully awake, he noticed that his wife was stirring by his side. He opened his eyes and saw a beam of light falling like a golden cactus leaf from the door. Jumping out of bed in his bare feet, he groped for his shirt and trousers on a box by the bed. Then he put on his shoes, which had no laces, and a dirty cap. He took a box of matches from his pocket and lit an oil lamp.

In the room there was a stifling atmosphere, heavy and sour, made up of dampness, acrid sweat and poverty. Felipe turned and let his eyes rest on his wife's body. She was lying face downwards with her head between her crossed arms. She was half covered by a counterpane of artificial silk, faded and full of patches. One of her calves were showing and a fly buzzed around it a moment before settling. By her side, a newly born child was sleeping, its legs drawn up and arms tucked in, in the position it had had in its mother's womb. The other three children were huddled together in a cot in front of which three rickety chairs had been placed so they would not roll out. One of them, after turning over, began an inarticulate song. Felipe, using his big rough hands with incredible gentleness, shook the child slowly and patted its bottom. It gave a long sigh and then was silent.

The tenement was coming to life at the call of the morning. There was the sound of a metal shutter being pushed up. Then in the distance the grinding of a tram. And immediately after that, the roar of a motor and the strident sound of a horn. A man doubled over in a hoarse, tearing cough, ended with a coarse clearing of his throat. Through the closed door filtered the slip-slop of slippers on the floor. A child's voice rang out happily and a man's voice answered. There was a pause, then the child's voice sounded, jubilant with astonishment; "Dad, see how the dog's barking at you."

Felipe took up the basket which contained his fishing tackle – lines, hooks, sinkers, a can for water – and put it under his arm. He gave a last glance at the cot where the children were sleeping and left the room.

Outside the door, he met an old woman, so old, wrinkled and consumed that she seemed only the shadow of a woman. "And how's Ambrosio?" he said.

The woman screwed her face into an expression of anguish: "Bad, bad, my son. Merse went for a doctor at the hospital, but he wouldn't come and said something about not being on duty. And now I'm waiting for him. I think Ambrosio is going to die."

"You can never tell. Maybe he'll see us all buried," said Felipe in an effort to cheer the old woman up.

The circumstantial evocation of death, however, had clouded his thoughts. And suddenly, as he went on his way he realised that he was remembering an incident he had experienced the previous evening. Provoked by one of those acts of injustice that can turn the most quiet tempered man into a murderer, it could have had tragic consequences. It had all started over a question of sharks fins. For some time, Felipe, like the other fishermen of La Punta and Casa Blanca, had avoided catching sharks. A decree from the President of the Republic had given the monopoly to a private company which, although it could not take full advantage of its privileges, was trying to exploit individual fishermen.

Up to that time, many poor families along the coast had depended on shark fishing to make a living. A Chinese on Zanja Street bought shark fins and tails, salted them and sold them in San Francisco, for these articles, along with swallows' nests and sturgeon soup are some of the most highly valued items in Chinese cooking. He paid two dollars for a set of fins, and this was very good business for the fishermen, since they also kept the rest of the fish. Out of its spine they made walking sticks, which looked like ivory; the teeth were sold as good luck charms, and the heads, dried, were sold as souvenirs to American tourists.

And then, unexpectedly, had come that wretched decree, which had put the Chinese out of business. It did not seem too bad at first when the whole matter was largely theoretical. Agents from the Shark Fishing Company arrived and made the fishermen an offer which seemed reasonable enough. They would buy the sharks and pay according to their length. They spoke eloquently and fast, so much so that the fishermen accepted their proposals with joy, even with gratitude. They very soon realised, however, that they had been tricked. Things were not as the agents had described them and for a fish to be worth a dollar, it had to be abnormally long. Also they had to hand over the entire fish with fins and tail. Not even a small piece of skin could be missing.

The fishermen, in the knowledge that they had been swindled, began to protest, asking for an increase in price. But the Company, without troubling to discuss the matter, referred to the presidential decree, and threatened them with prison. After this it began to exercise its rights tyranically. And the Company could count on the help of the Harbour Police which, stimulated by secret bribes, devoted itself more energetically to catching shark fishers than to catching water-front thieves and smugglers. The whole situation was intolerably unjust, especially as the Company made a profit from the entire fish. It sold the fins to Chinese, the bones to a button factory, the skin to the tanneries. An excellent lubricant was extracted from the livers and sold on the market as whale oil. And to make matters worse, the salted young sharks, only a few weeks old, were sold as "boneless codfish".

The result of this was that after a while the fishermen stopped catching sharks. And if by accident a shark got on to their lines, they killed it and left it, cut into pieces in the sea, rather than sell it to the Company for thirty or fifty cents.

Felipe had followed the behaviour of the rest. But as he said, "When things have to happen . . ." A few days previously, out at sea, he had not caught anything, not even a barracuda, which unscrupulous restaurant owners, in order to make a few cents, will serve at the risk of poisoning their customers.

And then suddenly a shark had started to swim round his boat. It was a hammer-head, about fifteen feet long, with long broad fins. Instinctively Felipe reached for his harpoon, but he was stopped by the idea that he was not supposed to catch sharks. So he watched the shark, which looked like a dark, flexible tree-trunk. Yes, it was like a tree-trunk, he thought. How much would it be worth? Felipe calculated that any Chinese in Zanja Street would pay at least two dollars for the fins and tail. He felt he should take those two dollars which the sea was offering so generously, to relieve his extreme poverty. Two dollars meant three good meals for his starving children. But then there were the Police and the agents for the Shark Fishing Company to think about.

On the water-front they were always on the look-out for any fisherman bringing in shark fins or tails. And if sometimes they merely confiscated the catch, at others they arrested the fishermen. And after that five dollars fine and they were not even allowed a defence. But two dollars were two dollars, and however hard he worked, it was possible that that day his wife would have nothing to cook. Fishing was always a game of chance and often one's luck did not depend on one's efforts. If only it were possible to make the fish bite! And those fins there, within the reach of his hands. Two dollars.

He made up his mind. Two dollars, for him. What the hell! Quickly, while he was preparing his harpoon, he threw out all the bait he had to keep the fish around. The shark surfaced, showing its stiff dorsal fins, its white under-belly flashing in the sunlight. When it had eaten the bait, it dived slowly, to emerge a few moments later behind the boat.

The harpoon, skilfully cast by Felipe, caught it in the neck and it struggled convulsively, churning up a whirlpool of water with its tail. A few blows with a mallet on the head were enough to quieten it down. Half an hour later its body, without fins or tail, sank, turning on itself to be eaten by its fellows in the depths of the sea.

Behind the mutilated body, like a silent protest, remained a wake of blood.

After tying the fins and the tail with a piece of cord, Felipe rowed towards the coast. He wanted to get ashore as soon as possible, to go early to China Town in search of a buyer. Perhaps with Chan, the owner of the *Canton*, he might strike a bargain. At worst he ought to exchange the fins for food.

And then suddenly fate, dressed in a blue uniform, arrived. Felipe had scarcely tied up his boat when he was startled by a harsh, sarcastic voice: "This time you can't deny it. I've caught you red-handed." And as he turned, his heart in a vice, he saw a policeman, smiling maliciously and pointing with his fore-finger at the fins and tail. After a moment's silence he added:

"I'll take those."

He bent down to pick them up. But he did not get to touch them because Felipe, jumping forward, grabbed them in his right hand.

"They are mine!" he muttered violently.

For a moment the policeman seemed astonished at meeting such behaviour. But he reacted quickly in an attempt to recover his authority:

"Come on, hand them over or I'll take you and the fins along with me."

Felipe looked at him carefully. He was a small man, skinny and ungainly. His precarious physique was in sharp contrast with his hectoring voice and the stance of a fighting-cock he had assumed. Felipe scowled and felt his arm muscles contract. And aware of his own strength and of the elasticity of his body, he said to himself:

"This fellow isn't even half a man."

In the meantime, a group of onlookers had collected around him and the policeman.

"Hand them over or you'll be sorry."

"Give them to him," advised a voice, that of an old copper-faced fisherman. And changing his tone:

"Perhaps he can see a doctor with what he gets for them."

Felipe felt the weight of innumerable eyes fixed on him and he imagined the scornful smiles and ironical comments with which the witnesses of the scene would taunt him afterwards. And apart from this, the feeling that he was being made the object of an intolerable injustice goaded him on to disobedience, whatever the consequences may be.

"I'm waiting. Are you going to hand them over or not?"

The bullying voice of the policeman was angry and threatening.

"Neither of us gets them," Felipe said suddenly. And whirling them round his head, he threw the fins into the sea.

The policeman, shaking with rage, ordered him to come to the harbour Station. But Felipe, partly overcome with fury, partly out of pride, refused to allow himself to be arrested. Nobody could foretell the outcome of the scene. But, fortunately, an army officer who had come up, intervened. In an authoritative voice he ordered the policeman to control himself and told Felipe to allow himself to be taken to the station.

"You had better go. The policeman has to do his duty."

Felipe protested, gave reasons. The policeman was going to beat him.

"And I'm not going to take it. If he hits me . . ." and in his reticence there was an implicit threat.

Finally, he accepted a compromise. He would allow the lieutenant to arrest him, but not the policeman. The soldier, an exception to the rule, was a sensible man and agreed. The policeman also accepted the solution though unwillingly, because he considered his authority undermined. All the way to the station he was muttering threats.

And now, on his way to the sea-front, Felipe remembered it all. The policeman had not been satisfied, and would try to get his own back. He had got himself into a nasty business over those shark fins. When he reached the bar on the corner of Cuba and Carteles Streets, he saw the father of Congo, his fishing partner. He asked where Congo was and was told he had been on the beach for a long time.

He walked quickly. Suddenly, as he came round the old Maestranza de Artilleria, his eyes were filled with the sight of a blue uniform, standing on the sea-front.

"I'm in for it now. It's that cop" he thought and for a moment felt like turning back. Any one of his friends would tell you that he was afraid of nothing, neither men on land nor foul weather at sea. No, he was not afraid, but why take risks? Still he was ashamed he had felt like running away. So he went forward resolutely, with a firm step, but with a nervous tension masking his basic anxiety.

He very soon discovered that his intuition had not deceived him. It was the same policeman, despotic and provocative like a fighting-cock. Congo had already got the boat against the wharf and was fixing the mast in readiness to unfurl the sail. As he came up, Felipe noticed the policeman was observing him.

"Foolishness," Congo was saying, continuing his conversation with the policeman.

"Foolishness?" said the policeman. "I'm boss around here. If that fellow gives any more trouble I'll beat his guts out."

Felipe, stinging under the crude threat, felt like hitting him, but he controlled himself.

"Look, man, lay off me. Wasn't yesterday's business enough for you?"

"Lay off you?" His voice was sarcastic, sharp like the point of a harpoon. "You'll soon find out what's what. The little lieutenant got you off last time, but you slip just once, and I'll beat the hell out of you."

Felipe still managed to keep himself under control. Speaking to Congo he complained: "Nice way to begin a day." The policeman jeered:

"Oh, you are all meek and mild now you've got nobody to defend you." There was such a concentration of sarcastic scorn in the voice that Felipe, beside himself with rage, jumped forward.

"To defend me against a thing like you ... you who ..."

The phrase stuck in his throat. His anger was choking him.

A minute which seemed a century passed. He tried to speak but his fury was like a knot in his throat. Then, unable to articulate a word, it occurred to him that his silence might be mistaken for cowardice. This thought shook him like a blow on the jaw. The blood that was choking him spread from his throat to his eyes, from his eyes to his head. And then, blind and deaf with fury, he advanced towards the policeman, his fists raised.

The dry crack of a shot disturbed the morning quiet. Felipe without understanding how or why suddenly felt himself stopped. Then he slumped down on the water-front, his eyes gazing at the sky. Against the limpid blue, he saw a long, shining cloud. "Like mother of pearl," he thought. And he remembered with extraordinary clarity the delicate sea-shells which decorated his childhood years. Some were perfectly white, others a more tender colour, a marvellous pale pink. He had lots of shells which he kept in boxes, mostly old shoe-boxes. "And now I must buy shoes for the kids because they are going around barefoot." This thought brought him back to reality. In a giddy succession of images he remembered his quarrel with the policeman. Did he actually hit him? An unspeakable lassitude, a sort of pleasant tiredness and feeling of comfort were relaxing his muscles. Suddenly he realised that he was dying. It was not lassitude or tiredness or comfort, it was his life leaving him. But he did not want to die, he could not die. It was his duty not to die. What would happen to his children? He must defend his life which was the life of his children, defend it with his hands, his feet, his teeth. His mouth was dumb as if it were already full of earth. But he was not dead yet. He tried to form a clear image of his children, but it kept slipping away, blurred and fleeting. In the distance, as if from miles away, he heard Congo's voice. Another voice. Other voices. He could not get the picture of his children clear. He could make out a vague, hazy outline as in a bad photograph. His heavy eyelids gradually closed. His mouth twisted in a desperate effort to speak. At last he was able to murmur: "My children ... my ... my ..."

He trembled violently and then remained motionless and silent, still and mute, his eyes staring at the sky.

On his chest over the left breast, almost invisible, there was a small red hole, about the size of a five-cent piece.

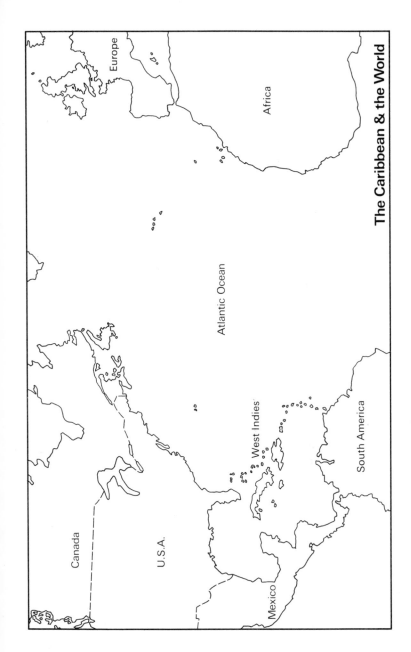

The Caribbean & the World

Europe

Africa

Atlantic Ocean

Canada

U.S.A.

West Indies

Mexico

South America

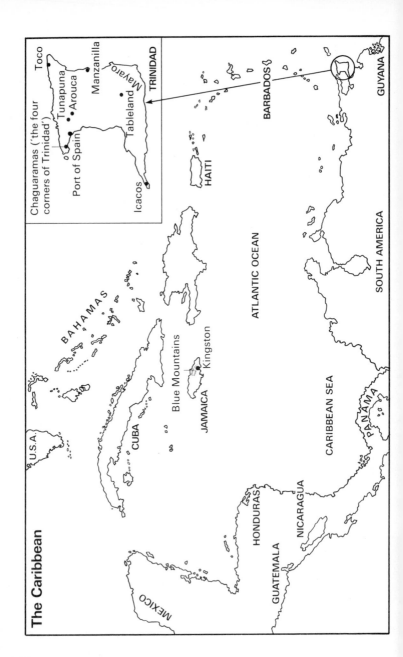

The Caribbean

U.S.A.

BAHAMAS

CUBA

MEXICO

GUATEMALA

HONDURAS

NICARAGUA

PANAMA

JAMAICA

Blue Mountains
● Kingston

CARIBBEAN SEA

HAITI

ATLANTIC OCEAN

BARBADOS

SOUTH AMERICA

GUYANA

TRINIDAD

Toco

Manzanilla

● Tunapuna
● Arouca

Mayaro

Chaguaramas ('the four corners of Trinidad')

● Port of Spain

Tableland

Icacos

The Caribbean:
a sequence of photographs

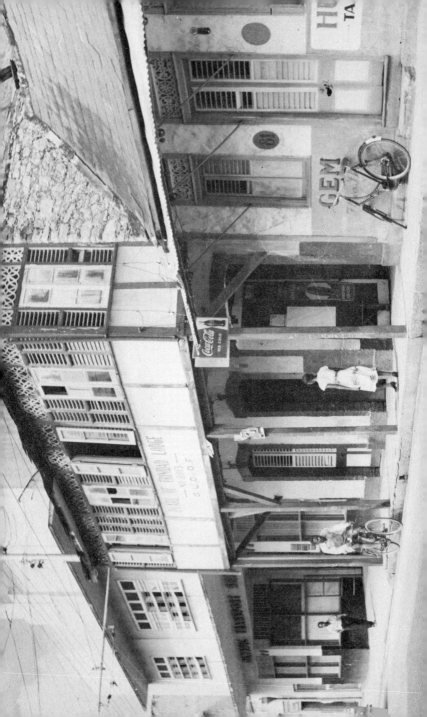

Points for Discussion and Suggestions for Writing

(Suggestions for writing are marked with an asterisk.)

Drunkard of the River

1   Consider how the author shows us the differing attitudes and concerns of the mother and son to Mano. Can you explain both their points of view?

2   Was Sona's final action inevitable? Discuss the reasons for your view.

*3   Write about the mother's feelings when she discovers the truth about her husband.

*4   Describe the next day, imagining you are Sona.

Hunters and Hunted

5   Describe the ways in which Tonic is different from his father and brothers.

6   Is there any significant connection between the jaguar's death and Tonic's? Do they affect us equally?

7   What do you understand by Tengar's remark "Is why folks like we does die so stupid"? How is it relevant to the story?

*8   Describe an occasion when you have been faced with the death of either somebody you knew, or of an animal.

*9   Putting yourself in the position of *one* of the characters, describe your feelings about hunting after this day's events.

The Tallow Pole

10   Do you consider this story to be humorous or sad, or both? Give reasons for your opinion.

11   Was it just the prizes that attracted people to the tallow pole?

*12   Write a story called "The Big Win".

* 13   Write a part of George Baker's autobiography.

A Village Tragedy

14   What are the elements of the story which make it specifically a *village* tragedy?

15   What are the reasons for the lack of friendship between Doctor Rushie and the Reverend Mackinnon?

16   Discuss the ways in which the characters are presented in the story.

* 17   Imagine you are Joseph. Tell the story he told to his sister Elvira the night of Ambrose Beckett's death.

* 18   Describe the result of the dispute over Thomas's and Sidney's inheritance; remember to include how they dealt with the Reverend Mackinnon.

The Red Ball

19   How is Bolan gradually accepted by the Woodford Square boys?

20   Do you think it is only the move to Port of Spain that has caused such a change in Bolan's father?

21   How do you think Bolan justifies himself in taking the money?

22   Do you think Bolan's father's statement is true, that "we love you like nothin' else in the whole whole world"?

* 23   Imagine you are Bolan's mother; describe her feelings about the red ball incident.

* 24   Follow the fortunes of the family in Port of Spain for the next few months. Write in diary form.

Blackout

25   Do you think that the cigarette incident is important in itself?

26   What do we learn about the man and woman from this encounter?

27 What do you understand by "in this country there are only men and women"?

*28 Two people of different nationalities meet by chance at a bus stop. Write the conversation that takes place.

The Enemy

29 Can you think of any particular reasons why the boy came to think of his mother as "the enemy"?

30 Why do you think the boy preferred his father?

31 Do you think the boy's relationship with his mother could improve?

32 What qualities make "The Enemy" into more than just a funny story?

*33 Have you any vivid memories of praise or pain from your childhood? Write about them.

*34 Write a conversation between the boy's father and mother in which they discuss his upbringing.

The Baker's Story

35 What does this story tell you about prejudice?

36 Does the first-person narrative in dialect add to the story?

37 How do we know what kind of person the narrator is?

38 Do you think this situation could only have happened in the West Indies? If not, try to think of local examples.

*39 Write the history of Yung Man Bakers from a customer's point of view.

*40 Write a story about exploitation.

The Raffle

41 Why did Mr Hinds first raffle his goat?

42 Do you think the boy's mother was justified in trying to get rid of the goat?

43 Why was Mr Hinds so angry when he heard of the goat's death?

44 Do you think the goat has any special significance in the story?

*45 Imagine you are a pupil in Mr Hinds's school. Write a detailed portrait of him.

*46 Write a fable or story called "The Goat".

The Visitor

47 What are the boy's first impressions of the man?

48 How is the boy's thinking affected by seeing the man and his mother together?

49 What kind of person is the boy's mother?

50 Do you feel sympathetic to the man in his curiosity about his son?

*51 Imagine you are the mother telling a neighbour about the visit.

*52 Have you ever visited or been visited by a long-lost relation? Describe the occasion and your feelings.

The Bitter Choice

53 What are the conflicting ideas discussed by the three men at the beginning of the story?

54 How does Leo's home life affect him?

55 Do you think Leo made the right choice?

56 Is compromise a good solution to problems generally?

*57 Write a poem or story entitled "Unemployed".

*58 Imagine a conversation between the three men the following day.

My Fathers Before Me

59 What are Dick's reasons for wanting to go to England?

60 Do you think the old woman was right to try to persuade him not to leave the West Indies?

61 In what ways is Vere important to the story?

62 What are Dick and his forefathers searching for in their travels?

*63 Describe Dick's feelings when he first arrives in England.

*64 Imagine you are an old person, and describe your past in another country.

Cane is Bitter

65 How has Romesh grown apart from his family?

66 How does Ramlal plan to re-unite Romesh with the family? What are Rookmin's views about it?

67 When Romesh returns to the village, how is he treated?

68 Do you think Romesh makes the right decision? Is education often the cause of the break-up of a family?

*69 Imagine you are Romesh. Write a letter home describing your life a few months later.

*70 Write an account of the events from Rookmin's point of view.

A Drink of Water

71 What kind of people were Rampersad and his wife?

72 How did Rannie get sick?

73 How did Manko and Sunny justify their actions? Do you think they were right?

74 What moral would you attach to the story?

*75 Imagine life in the village after the rain? What became of the Rampersads?

*76 Write a story for a newspaper, or a poem, called "Drought".

Shark Fins

77 What impression of Felipe's character do you gather from the story?

78 What drives Felipe to kill the shark?

79 Why does the policeman become so furious?

80 What are your feelings for Felipe at the end of the story?

*81 Imagine you are Felipe's wife or child – describe your reactions to his death.

*82 Write a description, poem or story called "Poverty".

The Authors

Michael Anthony was born in a small village in Trinidad. He went to a Roman Catholic school, and left at fifteen to work in a foundry. When he was twenty-two he emigrated to England, eventually becoming a teleprinter operator and working at the famous news agency, Reuter. He started writing articles, poems, and short stories, and his first was published in the main West Indian literary magazine, *Bim*, in 1959. Later he returned to Trinidad, working in the publications department of the big oil company, Texaco. Since then he has moved to work in the Trinidadian Ministry of Culture. He has published many novels, including *A Year in Sanfernando* and *Green Days by the River*. His short stories have been collected in *Cricket in the Road*.

Jan Carew left his home country of Guyana for America in 1941 when he was seventeen. He studied at university, then in Prague, and settled for a while in Holland, before coming to London. He now lives in England lecturing, acting, editing a local newspaper, and writing for radio and television as well as stories and novels.

Barnabas J. Ramon-Fortune, also from Trinidad, worked in the Trinidadian Civil Service until 1971, when he left to devote his time to writing. Many of his poems and short stories have been broadcast on the BBC programme "Caribbean Voices". He has twelve children himself, and many of his stories deal with parent – child relationships.

John Hearne was born in Canada, although his parents came from Jamaica, and he served in the Royal Air Force during the Second World War. He took a degree in History and Philosophy at Edinburgh University. His first novel was published in 1955, and he has continued to write. At the moment he is a Tutor in the Department of extra-mural studies at the University of the West Indies in Jamaica.

Ismith Khan was born in the capital of Trinidad in 1925. He started work as a reporter on the *Trinidad Guardian* before leaving for America, where he studied at Michigan University and the New York School for Social Research. He is now Director of Third World Studies at the University of California. His books include a story, based on his own life, of the difficulties of a boy struggling to make sense of the differences between his Indian grandfather's life and his own Western education.

Roger Mais died in 1955 at the age of fifty. He was born in Jamaica, where his mother was a teacher. During his life, he was concerned with the struggles for national independence. He has written two volumes of short stories, as well as three novels. He had earned his living as civil servant, timekeeper, agriculturalist, reporter, insurance salesman, and photographer.

V.S. Naipaul is undoubtedly the most famous writer of all those represented in this collection, and his novels and books of short stories are read all over the world. Indeed he has been called by some critics the finest novelist writing in English. He was born in Trinidad in 1932, of East Indian origin. His grandfather had come over from India, and his father was a journalist. After going to school in the Queen's Royal College there, he went to Oxford University. He has lived in England ever since. His first book was a collection of short stories that are linked by being set in a single street in Trinidad: Miguel Street. Since that he has written a number of brilliantly funny and thoughtful novels: *The Mystic Masseur*, *A House for Mr Biswas*, and others. His autobiography *The Middle Passage* describes the experience of someone leaving his home country. His latest volume of short stories is *A Flag in the Island*.

H. Orlando Patterson, who was born in Jamaica in 1940, studied at the University of the West Indies, and then took a PhD in Sociology at the London School of Economics, where he taught for a while before returning to the University of the West Indies. Apart from his short stories and two novels, he has published an important piece of research *The Sociology of Slavery*.

Clifford Sealy now manages a bookshop in Trinidad, where he was born in 1927. He completed his education at St Luke's College, Exeter, and worked in England for many years as a free-lance journalist for the BBC. He now edits a literary Quarterly of West Indian Writing, called *Voices*.

Karl Sealy comes from Barbados, and since 1952 has had nineteen stories published in *Bim*.

Samuel Selvon, another of the famous names in this collection, was born in 1924 of Indian parents, and lived in Trinidad. During the war he worked as a wireless operator in the Royal Naval Reserve, and then edited a weekly collection of Caribbean poetry and prose for the *Trinidad Guardian*. He started publishing his own writing, and in 1950 came to Britain. Since then he has published many novels and short stores. *Lonely Londoners*, is a very funny and well-known novel, and his collection of short stories *Ways of Sunlight* was published in 1957. He has written plays for the BBC, and received many awards.

Enrique Serpa is the oldest writer in this collection, having been born in Cuba in 1899. He wrote in Spanish, and this is a translation (by G.R. Coulthard).

The West Indies:
a brief historical note

The groups of islands between the Atlantic Ocean and the Caribbean Sea are mostly volcanic, often with high peaks. The climate is hot and wet, and the crops grow rapidly, often allowing two crops a year. The earliest inhabitants who settled and grew crops were the Arawaks and the Caribs (whose name was given to the sea: Caribbean). These people, known in general by the word "Amerindians", inhabited many of the islands for centuries. The Arawaks were reputed to be peaceful and the Caribs warlike. They had fully developed, if modest, societies, with their own culture, art, and agriculture. Their main crop was the shrub cassava, the roots of which are ground to make meal for bread, and for tapioca. They did not use metal weapons.

At the end of the fifteenth century the islands were "discovered" by the Europeans sailing with Columbus in search of the Indies, which explains why Europeans have always called the islands the "West Indies". These travellers realised that the lands would produce good crops, that there would be plenty of land, and that money could be made. There was also a hope that gold would be found. During the seventeenth and eighteenth centuries each of the main European countries captured various of the islands, often fighting with other countries so that some islands changed hands from the French to the Spanish or to the British, many times.

The original inhabitants were almost entirely wiped out by the fighting and by the diseases newly introduced from Europe. It is amazing to realise that an entire people could be removed in this way, only a few Amerindians surviving. The Europeans did not really *settle* these islands, but used them as reservoirs of money-earning crops for the home countries. Some families would go out to live permanently, and there were some poor among them, but mostly the Europeans were too few actually to work the land: they had come to exploit it. They therefore looked elsewhere for workers, and in the seventeenth and eighteenth centuries brought captured people from Africa, to work as slaves, living in very poor conditions. Their families and their village friendships were deliberately broken up, so that they would be easier to control. During this period the islands lived entirely by exporting crops such as sugar cane and coconuts. and no attempts were made to run the countries so that any benefit came to the islands. The colonies were there to serve the home country back in Europe.

In the early nineteenth century many people came to hate slavery and the use of human beings as if they were objects to be bought and sold. Britain legally abolished slavery in 1834, and gradually the other ruling countries did the same. Where they could, the freed slaves left their old masters and set up on their own, if possible leaving the land for the towns. Where then would the workers be found for the sugar cane fields or the coconut harvests, both of which depended on large numbers of unskilled labourers? After trying various countries of the world, the British brought labourers from India, under contract to work for five years. They came from poor parts of India; their fares were paid; they were housed in specially built wooden "barracks"; their conditions were carefully looked after by British officials. After five years, they had the choice of a free passage back, or a small piece of land of their own. This system went on for much of the nineteenth century.

In the first half of the twentieth century, up to the Second World War (in which the British islands supplied troops for the allied armies), the countries were ruled as "colonies" by the European countries that "owned" them. Although those countries did a great deal to improve conditions in the islands, running schools, transport systems, law courts, the police, and so on, the islands were seen as "colonies", whose main job was to produce cheap goods for the mother country, or to act as a guaranteed market for the manufactured products of that country. Not very much was done to build the West Indian countries up, to modernise their industry, or to develop them in the ways required for life in the modern industrial world.

After the war there was a considerable move towards self-governing independence, and, indeed, the great rise in the number of writers producing stories about the West Indies was part of this new spirit. Self-government, industries, and an economy of their own led the islands to want to develop local arts and not keep studying and reading the old European writers of the past. Jamaica was the first to be independent in 1962, then Trinidad and Tobago, and Barbados in 1966.

The society described in these stories reflects the West Indian world during this period of development. The new industrialisation, the tourist industry, and the development of a self-sufficient economy are hardly shown in these stories. But the

148

tensions between the generations that result from speedy changes will be felt. So will the tensions, usually resolved, between the many races. Each island is different, but there are often the descendants of Europeans of different original nationalities and languages, of orientals, of those whose ancestors came from Africa, and those whose ancestors came from India. These last two groups, in particular, are the largest, and although they live and work together, their cultures, family life occupations, and life styles are usually very different.

These stories, mostly written in the 1950s and 1960s, are by writers proud of their country's life, and able to draw inspiration from their own backgrounds. The Caribbean has created a literature of its own, but one which can be enjoyed throughout the world.

Further Reading

These books are recommended for student readers and secondary school libraries.

Novels

ANTHONY, MICHAEL, *A Year in Sanfernando*, Heinemann Caribbean Writers Series

ANTHONY, MICHAEL, *Green Days by the River*, Heinemann Caribbean Writers Series

CAREW, JAN, *Black Midas*, Longman Caribbean

HARRIS, WILSON, *The Sleepers of Roraima*, Faber and Faber (An attempt to bring to life the ancient past of the West Indies in the time of the Caribs. Three long interlinked stories, in each of which a boy gradually discovers the myths of the Caribs.)

JONES, PATRICK MARION, *Pan Beat*, Columbus Press, Trinidad (Set in a Trinidadian school, and all about the forming of a steel band and the loyalties of the young people.)

NAIPAUL, V.S., *The Mystic Masseur*, Heinemann Caribbean Writers (A comic satire of the rise to fame of a mystic.)

REID, VIC, *Sixty-Five*, Longman Caribbean (The rebellion of Maroant Bay, Jamaica, in 1865, seen through the eyes of a young boy.)

REID, VIC, *The Young Warriors*, Longman Caribbean (Four boys protect their village from an attack by the British.)

SALKEY, ANDREW, *Hurricane*, Oxford University Press (A family caught up in the dangerous hurricane that swept the islands.)

SELVON, SAMUEL, *The Lonely Londoners*, Longman Caribbean (The complications of being an immigrant in London in the 1950s.)

Short Stories

ANTHONY, MICHAEL, *Cricket on the Road*, Heinemann Caribbean Writers

NAIPAUL, V.S., *Miguel Street*, Heinemann Caribbean Writers

NAIPAUL, V.S., *A Flag on the Island*, André Deutsch; Penguin

SELVON, SAMUEL, *Ways of Sunlight*, Longman Caribbean

Collections

GRAY, CECIL, (*ed*) *Response*, Nelson
SALKEY, ANDREW, (*ed*) *West Indian Stories*, Faber and Faber

Poetry

RAMCHAND, KENNETH, AND GRAY, CECIL, (*ed*) *West Indian Poetry*,
Longman Caribbean
WALMSLEY, ANNE, (*ed*) *The Sun's Eye*, Longman Caribbean

History and Geography

ANTHONY, MICHAEL, *Profile Trinidad*, Macmillan Education (A
clear and fairly short account of the history of one island.)
AUGIER, ROY; GORDON, SHIRLEY; HALL, DOUGLAS; AND RECKORD,
MARY, *The Making of the West Indies*, Longman Caribbean
(An economic and social and political history of the West
Indies, 1492–1963.)
BRATHWAITE, EDWARD, (*ed*) *The People Who Came*, Longman
Caribbean (A three-volume secondary school history of the
New World.)
MACPHERSON, JOHN, *Caribbean Lands*, Longman Caribbean (A
geography of the West Indies.)

For advanced students, there is a scholarly literary study of the
origins and growth of West Indian fiction: *The West Indian Novel
and its Background*, by KENNETH RAMCHAND, Faber and Faber.

Acknowledgements

We are grateful to the following for permission to reproduce copyright material:

Jonathan Cape Ltd. for the story 'Blackout' by Roger Mais from *And Most Of All Man* reprinted by permission of Mrs. Jessie Taylor, sister and Executrix of the author; The author for his story 'Hunters and Hunted' by Jan R. Carew from *Images* published by Thomas Nelson & Sons Ltd; Andre Deutsch Ltd. for the stories 'The Enemy', 'The Baker's Story' and 'The Raffle' by V. S. Naipaul from *A Flag On The Island*; Author's Agent for the story 'A Village Tragedy' by John Hearne from *Atlantic Monthly* 1960; The author for his story 'The Red Ball' by Ismith Khan from *New Writing in Caribbean* by A. S. Seymour; The author for his story 'The Visitor' by H. Orlando Patterson; The author for his story 'The Tallow Pole' by Barnabas J. Ramon-Fortune from *West Indian Stories* ed. by A. Salkey; The author for his story 'My Fathers Before Me' by Karl Sealy from *West Indian Stories* ed. by A. Salkey; The author for his story 'The Bitter Choice' by Clifford Sealy from *Caribbean Prose* ed. by A. Salkey; The author for his stories 'Cane Is Bitter' and 'A Drink Of Water' by Sam Selvon from *Ways of Sunlight* published by Hart-Davis, MacGibbon.

We regret that we have been unable to trace the copyright holders of the following stories and would appreciate any information that would enable us to do so:

'Drunkar. Of The River' by Michael Anthony, 'Shark Fins' by Enrio. Serpa, translated by Prof. G.R. Coulthard.

. grateful to the following for permission to reproduce graphs:

Bolt, pages 117 and 118; Adrian Boot, pages 116, 127, 129, and 137; Syd Burke, pages (i), (iii), 115, 122, 132 and 133; mera Press, pages 123 (photo Patrick Lichfield), 125 (photo nox Smillie), 128, 136 (photo Lennox Smillie) and Cover to Patrick Lichfield); Douglas Dickins, pages 120, 121 and usan Griggs Agency, page 126; Guyana Embassy, pages 134; David Wright, page 119.

lso grateful to Sarah Ray, who devised the questions for nd discussion